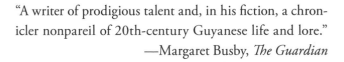

"A writer of prodigious talent and, in his fiction, a chronicler nonpareil of 20th-century Guyanese life and lore."
—Margaret Busby, *The Guardian*

"A beautiful writer and an unforgettable book."
—Salman Rushdie

"Move *Crime and Punishment* from the slums of St. Petersburg to the slums of Georgetown, Guyana, and you'll have something like *The Murderer*."
—Michael Harris, *Los Angeles Times Book Review*

"Roy Heath is one of those gifted writers whose prose seems at once spare and rich . . . The compression, the exotic setting, the faint, persistent threat of violence—the combination works like a troubling dream . . . [A] remarkable novel."
—Adam Begley, *Boston Review*

"Simply one of the most astonishingly good novelists of our time."
—Edward Blishen

THE MURDERER

THE MURDERER

ROY HEATH

McNally Editions

New York

McNally Editions
52 Prince St, New York 10012

ISBN: 978-1-946022-29-5
Ebook: 978-1-946022-35-6

Designed by Jonathan D. Lippincott

1   3   5   7   9   10   8   6   4   2

To wife, mother and sister—

the endlessly forbearing

BOOK ONE

ONE

Galton had been as a boy tall for his age, unlike his elder brother. In nearly every other respect they differed as well. Selwyn, carefree, almost insolent in his self-assurance, had striven for nothing but had received—so it seemed to Galton—more than his share of success and adulation. The freedom Selwyn enjoyed, as if of right, had not been wrung from his mother, nor had been granted by way of a reward. He simply went out when he wished, brought home the friends he chose and generally displayed a degree of independence reserved for husbands of adoring wives.

Galton had, at the age of nine or ten, learned to adapt himself to the bit between his teeth. Assured at first that he was too young to go out, as he grew older his mother claimed that he had developed a weak constitution. One day when a girl from his school came to call for him his mother laughed as if it were a big joke; Galton remained inside, his eyes closed tight in shame. But by the time he was in his early teens he no longer felt humiliated at such treatment and would have been surprised if a stranger had sympathised with him.

Selwyn was Galton's hero, protector and the agent through whom he learned what went on in the world outside the house and school. Galton seized on every suggestion that he might be included in Selwyn's activities and listened avidly to the latter's accounts of his exploits.

On Sundays Galton went to church at least once. Mrs Flood allowed him to choose whether he would attend the morning or the evening service, and usually he went in the morning "to get it over with." One particularly important Sunday when the harvest gifts were displayed beneath the pulpit Galton put off his church visit until the evening. At twenty minutes to seven, just as the church bells began ringing, his mother went off, warning him not to be late. But while he was getting ready Selwyn beckoned him to come to the kitchen. He joined his brother, his heart racing in anticipation as to what the latter had in store for him. Selwyn stood back and allowed him to take his place at the chink in the window. Through the gap Galton saw their neighbour, a former vaudeville dancer now in her sixties and mother of several children. She was dancing by herself, dressed in an old costume that left a strip of her waist exposed. Galton could not keep his eyes off the folds of dry skin trembling between the rows of glistening sequins; and when later he confessed to the disgust aroused in him by the woman's lecherous gestures, Selwyn told him mockingly that he ought to study for the ministry. And then, shaking his hips in a passable imitation of the dancer's number, Selwyn kept repeating, "I gwine wind like a twine!" a quotation from an old vaudeville song he had often heard the woman singing.

Galton remembered the father of his childhood as a jovial man who in later years fell silent whenever he came home at night. His heroic efforts to avoid quarrelling with his wife were not always successful. He only asked that she spare him the embarrassment of picking a quarrel with him while his friends were there, a concession she invariably granted. So that, on Boxing Day or Old Year's night when it was his turn to entertain, she would shut herself in the bedroom or go out, allowing them the run of the drawing-room and gallery. Then Galton's father made innumerable trips to the refrigerator in the dining-room to replenish their rum glasses with ice. And, if she was out, his tongue would loosen under the influence of the liquor and it would not be long before he invited his friends to sing his favourite song:

> One night when the moon was mellow
> Rosita met young Manello;
> He held her like this, the little miss,
> And stole a kiss, the fellow.

And at such a moment Galton, inexplicably, would swell with sympathy for his father.

Once, on a visit with him to a friend's house in the country—it was only in his father's company that he was permitted by his mother to go on any lengthy excursions—he was surprised to discover that his father was as much at home in the country as in town. He slipped readily into creolese, embraced the women of the family and generally behaved as if he had been born and brought up in a village. When he opened the bottle of rum he had brought he poured out a small amount on to the floor boards "to the spirits of the dead," he declared. Only then did he pour himself a shot into the glass he was holding in his left hand.

Indeed, the incident that Galton recalled most clearly as being associated with that visit concerned an infant, who had been creeping naked about the house. The child messed on the floor and the host promptly called his wife to wipe up the filth. Galton's father, having placed his hand of cards face down on the table, picked up the child and addressed it with terms of endearment.

The two persons Galton admired most—his father and brother—shared the same facility in their relations with others. He himself dared not cultivate an affection lest it reared up and attacked him; nor could he express his dislike for a person for fear that the intensity of his disapproval might seem absurd, and with time he brushed aside every impulse to display any tender emotion towards the members of his family.

The sustained humiliation at his mother's hands, the inability to match his father and brother in any skill, imbued Galton with a distaste for competition of all kinds and often led him to indulge in fantasies of self-abasement. Thus he frequently saw himself driving a dray-cart through streets lined with his relations and acquaintances, who were pointing in his direction each with their mouth covered with one hand.

Apparently, all that remained of an impulsive temperament was a strong disapproval of any attempt on his mother's part to challenge his father's authority. The night she attempted to lock her husband out Galton waited until the whole family was asleep, then slid down to the ground by means of the papaw tree outside the window. He spent the rest of the dark hours brooding under the house.

When his father died the week after he had gone to work in his brother's pharmacy, Galton decided to make a bid for freedom. However, his mother's hold over him, uncertain in her eyes but very real to Galton, kept him by her side. He was already nineteen.

Yet it was in this period that he struck up a friendship with Winston. They had known each other at secondary school, but at that time Winston, who had his own circle of friends, always seemed busy. Likeable and generous, he made an immediate impression on Mrs Flood, whom he won over by his attentiveness. When he plucked some wild flowers and, half-jokingly, presented them to her, she took the offering so seriously that the servant was made to place them in a vase of water. He even brought round his woman friend, whom he introduced to Mrs Flood as the girl he was going to marry. Jessie and Galton's mother talked until Winston was ready to go, when Mrs Flood made him promise to bring her again.

But Mrs Flood took ill and died soon afterwards, about a year after her husband's death. At the end of a suitable period of mourning Galton made up his mind to take the first step towards independence. He bought a ticket for the Guyana Sports Club dance and, on the night, presented himself at the desk where the tickets were being collected. However, the thought of going past these men and actually entering a dance hall was so daunting, Galton drew back, returning later, when the entrance was packed with people eager to get in. Upstairs, the dancers could be seen, thrusting their arms and shoulders forward in sudden, violent gestures. Galton could not dance and the elaborate movements did not appear easy to master. Nevertheless, he would go and watch. But when he stepped forward he could neither raise his hand nor open his mouth.

"Yes?" asked the collector.

Galton turned tail and made his way through the throng, seized by a sort of panic. Earlier, it had not been the absence of people that frightened him, as he then thought; he was simply incapable of entering a building where, according to his mother, people engaged in public love-making. Dancing was sinful, unless the dancers were married. Walking slowly towards the big gate which led on to the road he heard the band strike up a slow, sentimental piece and turned round to see the silhouettes of couples with their faces pressed together.

In the weeks that passed Galton developed such hostile feelings towards the house he shared with his brother that he announced his intention of going away and taking his part of the proceeds of the inheritance of movable property.

"What you're going to do with the money?" Selwyn asked.

"I'm going to Linden."

"What for?"

"It could just as well be Bartica or New Amsterdam."

"Oh," muttered Selwyn. "Look, why not study something? To waste. . . ."

"I just want to get away!" Galton snapped in a high-pitched voice his brother recognised as the sign to bring their conversation to an end.

Selwyn, sole executor of their mother's estate, advanced him two thousand dollars. When the money gave out Galton intended to find a job and begin life anew, as it were.

TWO

The day after his arrival in Linden Galton sought company in the cake shops of the arcade near the waterfront; but it was only several days later that he plucked up the courage to ask a man he frequently met about cheaper lodgings.

"Go to Mr Burrowes. He last lodger lef', I t'ink."

Galton usually avoided the cake shop owned by Burrowes, on account of its lack of privacy. Everything was public there, the discussions, the gossip, the scrutiny to which strangers were subjected, the loud talking and even the accounts Mr Burrowes kept of his customers' debts.

He put off his enquiry when he saw the crowd of people and heard the animated conversation, but came back late at night, a little before closing time.

Mr Burrowes thought that Galton wanted to buy something.

"Got to catch the last boat, boy. Come tomorrow."

"It's about lodgings. I hear you let a room."

"Lodgings?" asked Mr Burrowes. "Come in, ne?"

"About your boat," Galton reminded him.

"Oh, I can always get a late one," he replied.

Inside. Mr Burrowes took a bottle from the shelf, but Galton objected that he did not drink.

"Nothing wrong with that," observed Mr Burrowes. "My grandfather didn't drink, and he still lived to a ripe old age."

He replaced the bottle, all the while trying to formulate a sensible question. After all he could not accept just anyone to live in his house.

"From Georgetown, eh?"

"Yes," Galton answered.

"Why you come to these parts?"

"I felt like it."

"Oh, I can see you're decent. It's. . . . You see I've got a grown-up daughter. I can see you're decent, mind you. Decent and quiet. You go to church?"

"No, not any more."

"Mm . . . my grandfather didn't go to church either. He was the one that lived so long. Where're you staying now?"

"At the guest-house."

"Ah," said Mr Burrowes. "Expensive, eh? I suppose it'll be all right."

With that the bargain was struck, without any discussion as to a price. Galton agreed to meet Mr Burrowes the following day at seven in the evening.

Galton climbed out of the launch and took his suitcase from Mr Burrowes who paid the boatman before joining him on the wharf.

"It's not far," the latter said, pointing beyond the wharf.

Although night had fallen the other bank, a short distance away, was still clearly visible, marked with the bobbing lights of boats tied up along a more extensive wharf. The size of the houses in Wismar betrayed the fact that the township supported a less thriving community than McKenzie, the other half of Linden on the opposite side of the river. Mr Burrowes's house, in a side street just off the main road, was trim and well-maintained.

"It's not like a Georgetown place," he said apologetically, "but it's my own, mortgage-free and all."

Galton gratefully put his suitcase down in the drawing-room and waited for his host, who asked him to take a seat in a wicker chair, after promising to be back at once.

There was no gallery, as in the Georgetown cottages. One stepped directly from the stairs into the drawing-room, where a shabby Berbice chair, its foot-rest stretched full-length, stood in the company of three straight-backed chairs.

From inside came a young woman's voice, then all was quiet once more. Just as he thought that Mr Burrowes was coming back to join him the sound of his steps receded. A woman's singing rose from an adjoining yard and bits of indistinct conversation mingled with the bawling voice reminded Galton of his own home in Kitty.

Galton felt at once that he would be happy in this house, which belonged to a stranger he hardly knew and someone else whom he had not even seen.

Mr Burrowes finally came back out, rubbing his hands.

"We took her by surprise," he said in a low voice. "My daughter Gemma."

The young lady came forward, her right hand outstretched, and as she shook Galton's hand cast a sidelong glance at her father.

"We're hungry, girl," Mr Burrowes said.

"All right," she replied. "You take Mr Flood to the room."

Then, to Galton she said, "Pa didn't tell you how small the room is?"

When she left them Mr Burrowes winked at Galton. "I don't know what I'd do without her. Come this way."

Galton followed his host into a tiny room.

"I bet it wasn't so small at the guest-house. Anyway, in a few days you'll know if you like it."

Mr Burrowes withdrew and Galton went to the window to look down into the yard. On the other side of the fence was a range yard from the windows of which feeble rays of light shone. Beyond the range rose the roofs of cottages against a background of mounds which Galton was to learn later was the waste from the bauxite excavations. He would have liked to overlook the river and watch the launches coming and going. Turning round to survey his own room he saw through an open door leading to another bedroom a shelf full of books.

There was a knock on the door.

"You're ready?" came the young woman's voice.

Galton opened up, followed her to the dining-table, where he sat in a chair opposite Mr Burrowes. Immediately Gemma began ladling soup into the deep plates for her father, for the lodger and for herself in turn. Surprised that the sharing of food had begun before grace Galton involuntarily bowed his head before starting.

"What was the guest-house like?" asked Mr Burrowes.

"Pa, you know what the guest-house is like," Gemma remarked swiftly, and in her voice there was less censure than the desire to remind him to be sparing with his words.

"Girl, I'm just trying to make conversation."

"I don't mind," replied Galton, intrigued by the fraternal manner of the exchange.

"There's little to tell," continued Galton, "after such a short time. It's the first time I've been out of Georgetown."

"I thought you were from Kitty," said Gemma.

"It's a part of Georgetown now. All that divides the two is the railway line."

"We hear all the news here, you know," said Mr Burrowes. "We get the *Graphic*. And besides most of the people working in Linden are not from these parts. It's only this side of the river that's got any soul. But you think they'd spend any money on us? Oh, no! Everything's for McKenzie."

Gemma uncovered the bowl of rice and served the two men.

"I suppose you're thinking what we do for entertainment round here," said Mr Burrowes. "There's where all of it is, on the other side of Linden." He pointed with his knife across the river.

"You don't like it there, then?" asked Galton.

Mr Burrowes hesitated. "I get a living out of it."

The host continued talking and for Galton the meal was like one slow unwinding, fed by the presence of this man and his daughter, who spoke to each other like equals.

When Gemma cleared the plates away she left the men talking at table.

"Some women're born for marriage," Mr Burrowes confided. "She's like her mother. You see that woman that does run the guest-house, it's not hers, you know. There was a big scandal and I had to give evidence because I knew her husband. Gemma doesn't like me to talk about it."

"I didn't mind you asking," said Galton.

With Gemma's departure from the table Mr Burrowes sensed that Galton was not as attentive as he had been.

As his host got up Galton asked, "Who reads all those books in the other room?"

"Not me. It's Gemma. Don't know what she sees in them. You read a lot?"

"In fits, you know," Galton answered.

"What time you go to bed?"

"Elevenish."

"Mm," muttered Mr Burrowes. "Want to come out with me? It's one of those nights. I just don't feel like staying home."

Mr Burrowes took him round to friends and relatives in Wismar, "so that you'll know who to say hello to." And on the way back Galton answered questions about his family and his past life; but while talking his thoughts were fixed on Mr Burrowes's daughter.

Would she be in bed when they got back? he wondered.

Everything she did seemed extraordinary.

"You know what the guest-house is like," she had said. Was she not aware of the effect her voice produced? Were most women like this? At school the opportunities to speak to girls had been few and, in any case, they only responded favourably to the boys who were forward. The one girl who had taken an interest in him ignored him after her visit to his home.

"Why you're walking so fast?" asked Mr Burrowes.

"Am I?" said Galton.

Mr Burrowes picked a lime from the lime tree in his back yard to make two glasses of swank for Galton and himself. They then sat at the front of the house sipping their drink and listening to the radio, but soon afterwards Mr Burrowes fell asleep in his Berbice chair, his head on one side.

Galton went outside where, from the porch, he could see across the river. Here and there electric bulbs flickered like lamps, while on the near side only a solitary light shone on the wharf, to be put out, no doubt, when the last boat came in.

The people he had been introduced to by Mr Burrowes confirmed his favourable impression of Wismar. He had left Georgetown because he could no longer bear to live in the house of his birth; and now he desired to remain in Wismar on account of a man whom he met by chance and those connected with him.

THREE

Galton was in love. He spent his days watching for the boat that brought Gemma from work across the river, and his nights hoping that she would not go out again. For the week he had been lodging there she had hardly addressed him a word, nor, by any sign or action, given him encouragement. But he cared little about her neglect, seeing in his passion a release from all the constraints of years gone by.

Sometimes he felt that relations between herself and her father were strained, and only kept within the bounds of amity by his presence. But he feared that any manifestations of interest on his part would be interpreted as inquisitiveness. Even when Mr Burrowes made allusions that clearly invited a question Galton held back, preferring the former to confide in him without prompting.

The curious notion took hold of him that if there was actually a quarrel between Mr Burrowes and Gemma, he, Galton, would be asked to leave. He found himself listening for every silence between them, observing their glances and analysing their remarks for evidence of irritation.

The first day of the fourth week, when Galton came back from a walk across the mounds it seemed to him that his bed had been made with extra care; and that night he found that the mosquito netting was down. It was Gemma's way of suggesting that he use it. This evidence of her concern so touched Galton that he bought her a novel from a shop in McKenzie and at dinner presented it to her.

"You got it for me?" she asked.

"I wasn't sure if you'd like it."

"I do. I've read some of his books," she answered, not taking her eyes off him for a second.

"It's the first time I've seen that look in her eye," said Mr Burrowes.

Galton forced a smile, intensely embarrassed by his host's intervention.

"Most other men would've waited until I was out," remarked Mr Burrowes jokingly.

"Oh," said Galton, shrugging his shoulders in an attempt to hide his confusion.

From then on there developed between the two young people an intimacy of gestures. Galton agreed to offers of more food with a nod while Gemma indicated by a smile that she was retiring for the night. In the morning she waved from the foot of the stairs and he answered by raising his hand slightly. At night they often sat in the dark, usually in silence. But sometimes she spoke of herself. Her mother had died when she was five and it was her father who, single-handed, brought her up, showering her with reading matter so that she would not be bored.

One afternoon Galton met her by accident. As the little boat chugged in he turned his head and saw her sitting at the front, ahead of the dozen or so passengers. She smiled in a way she never did in the house, then suggested that as they were already out they might as well go for a boat ride.

"At this time?" asked Galton.

"You don't want to?"

"Yes. I didn't think we could get a boat."

"Oh, yes," she assured him.

He followed her to the other side of the wharf and up to a house further down the road.

"Wait here," she told him.

Galton waited for her, lost in admiration at her self-assurance. On looking up at the house again he saw her in conversation with a man who disappeared into the house for a while and then came back to join her.

Gemma sat down beside Galton, unaware of the fires she was kindling in his body. The impassive face of the boatman, the nearness of Gemma, the ever-increasing size of an approaching ship conspired to excite Galton to such a degree that he seized her hand. She only smiled, and he felt at that moment that all the doubts about himself had been washed away.

At home they said nothing to each other while they waited for Gemma's father to come back for dinner.

The first afternoon of the wet season, when the rain came roaring across the trees, Galton was finishing a letter to Winston. Soon the river was almost obscured by the downpour and the gutter in front of the house had disappeared under a rivulet of brown water. Gemma had not taken an umbrella with her. He remembered exactly her skirt and blouse, the handbag over her right shoulder and her empty hands. If the rain continued she would be marooned in the arcade, probably for hours.

Galton hesitated, his temptation to go and meet Gemma with an umbrella tempered by the forbidding prospect of searching for her among a crowd of people, most of whom would recognise him as a stranger. Besides, she might have gone to a friend's house or even stayed on at work. But, unable to bear the waiting, he set out with his large umbrella, leaving the unfinished letter in the drawer of his bedside table.

The half-empty boat barely touched the bank when the passengers began to disembark, impatient to get out of the rain. Galton noticed that only a few of them carried umbrellas, mostly too small to shelter them adequately.

His heart raced as the boat slowed down on approaching the other shore and the outline of shops appeared more distinctly through the rain. The passengers ahead of him seemed to be taking their time in stepping from the boat on to the logs embedded in the mud.

Should he pretend that he came to buy something he could not get in Wismar, that he only met her by chance? No. For once he would boldly declare his intentions. On the way to the arcade he rehearsed what he would say to her and did not notice that his shoes and the lower part of his trousers were becoming soaked.

Galton examined the faces of the people sheltering under the arcade, which in turn followed him as he went by, his umbrella pointed towards the ground. And when he reached the junction where the covered way opened out on to the street he was obliged to turn and make the trip once more. Then, hardly had he gone a few yards than he caught sight of her, leaning against a shop wall. She was smiling broadly at a young man who stood in front of her, entertaining her with his talk. Galton stared at them, oblivious of those around him, of the rain and the conversations, foundering in the swell of his jealousy. Her expression was bolder, her bodice seemed to display more of her delicate skin than it had that morning and her nipples stood out under her brassiere in a way he had never seen before.

"Galton!" Gemma cried out, on catching sight of him.

She introduced him to the young man, who addressed him familiarly as "friend."

"You've brought the umbrella!" she exclaimed, taking it from him.

"See you tomorrow," she told her companion and, opening the umbrella before they stepped out into the rain, turned round to wave to him.

"You're quiet," she whispered, cocking her head and looking up into his eyes. But he did not reply.

Guessing that he might have been jealous of the young man, Gemma, as soon as they were back in the house, kissed him first on one cheek, then on the other.

"Why don't you ever say what you think? It's not a crime, you know. There's nothing between him and me. We work in the same place, that's all . . . that's all."

His chagrin was dispelled at a stroke by her words and, in its place, there was shame, like the taste of red peppers. He drew her to him and kissed her. It was his first kiss, his first contact with a woman, which he had not sought, but desired passionately. Gemma yielded, drunk with the silence in the house and the pounding rain. But Galton drew away, mistrusting his indulgence.

Later that night when Gemma was in bed Mr Burrowes said to Galton, "You don't like independent women, eh?"

"I never thought of it," was his reply.

"Women," Mr Burrowes said reflectively, as if he had already given the matter much thought. "You're never free of them."

"You're free, aren't you?" asked Galton.

"Yes." he replied. And Galton did not know if the "Yes" was meant as an answer or a question. For the first time since he had been living there he felt a desire to question his host. There were things he would have liked to know about him and Gemma. Especially Gemma, who, hardly out of her teens, exerted a strange influence over her father. Although Galton had more than once caught a fleeting expression of exasperation on Mr Burrowes's face, he was content to do as his daughter wished, simply, it appeared, to please her. And yet, Galton thought, there was an element in their relationship which eluded him. At times he believed that Mr Burrowes could not stand Gemma; on the other hand the father undoubtedly needed the daughter's guiding hand, especially in the administration of his finances. It was she who made up his shop accounts on Saturdays and, so he told Galton, did his tax returns.

Galton's curiosity was to be satisfied soon afterwards when, the same week, he met the Walk-Man. This was a middle-aged man who frequented Mr Burrowes's shop in Linden and entertained everyone within earshot with his talk and mimicry. He claimed to be a descendant of Cuffy the slave leader and to have mastered the art of deducing a person's character from his walk. The skill had been handed down from generation to generation in his family, he said, and at present his eldest son was serving a most rigorous apprenticeship in the discipline. Those who called him Lie-Man rather than Walk-Man, were roundly abused and relegated to "the large band of idiots that plagued the earth."

When the Walk-Man met Galton at the shop, where he had gone on his way back from a trip to Georgetown, the company of customers clamoured for a diagnosis of the young man's character.

"Will you be so kind as to leave the shop, walk down the road and come back?" the Walk-Man requested.

Galton complied, regretting that he was fool enough to have come to the shop. He walked for about ten yards then turned back. The customers were standing on the forecourt watching Galton's legs, his hips and the way he moved his shoulders, while the Walk-Man held himself apart, never taking his eyes off Mr Burrowes's lodger.

"Well, le' we hear you now," said a customer, addressing the Walk-Man.

"He's running," replied the Walk-Man.

"How you mean?" another customer asked.

"He's running," repeated the Walk-Man, turning his back on the company and re-entering the shop.

"How he running when he walking?" pursued the first customer.

"He's running away, away from something," the Walk-Man declared.

Everyone turned to look at Galton, who smiled contemptuously. What right had these people to make him a part of their futile games, he thought. Oddly, his anger was directed at Mr Burrowes, who had kept quiet during the proceedings, but had never taken his eyes off him.

"What'm I running from?" asked Galton.

"Well . . . I'm not a magician. I'm a scientist. It's obvious from your walk you hate to face your problems. You prefer to run away," the Walk-Man answered.

Seeing that he was no match for the Walk-Man Galton searched desperately for a telling remark.

"You understand my character better than I do!" he exclaimed, pretending to be amused.

"Ah!" answered the Walk-Man. "If only everyone else knew that—about the impossibility of seeing oneself—we would stop beating our heads against a wall. . . ."

"You gone and vex the man," a third customer said, interrupting the Walk-Man. "Mister, let me buy you a drink," he offered, turning to Galton. "A Banks beer?"

Galton nodded. He never touched alcohol, but was glad that the customer had come to his rescue.

"No!" protested the Walk-Man. "I'll buy the beer! In fact you'll eat with me, at my house."

His voice was conciliatory and, embracing Galton, he said to the company, "Society of philistines! The vocabulary of contempt isn't wide enough to accommodate my opinion of you."

"Eh, eh, Lie-Man!" exclaimed a customer who had not yet spoken. "You conscience stinging you? Careful, mister, don't go in a rum-shop wit' he, 'cause he going start tying up he shoelace while you go through the door. He's the stingiest man in Linden."

The departure of the Walk-Man in Galton's company was accompanied by loud laughter.

The Walk-Man's house, raised no more than a couple of feet from the ground, was about ten minutes' walk from the shop. When they were at the gate he nudged Galton. "The wife's a battleaxe, but she looks after me, so don't say anything to offend her."

Galton followed him into the drawing-room, where the wife was sitting on the far side, her back to the door.

"So you come home after all," she said, half turning, so that Galton only saw her profile in the half-light.

"God!" he exclaimed, gaping at the Walk-Man's wife.

"What's the matter?" asked the Walk-Man, alarmed at Galton's expression.

His wife got up and came towards them and Galton, on seeing her more closely said. "I'm sorry. It's just that—in the dark and seeing you like that . . . you looked like my mother."

"That's all!" said the Walk-Man. "I thought you were going to have a fit. . . . My wife Mabel."

Mabel and Galton shook hands.

"He's eating with us, Mabel," her husband ventured.

"Oh, that's all right. I wish everybody you bring home look like him. Mister Galton, he does come home with all sorts of people he meet. Every crab-dog he pick up got to come home just so he can get a audience."

The Walk-Man stood by, smiling, but as soon as his wife disappeared in the back his expression changed and he said in a whisper: "I had to lock up my personality in a box to survive in this house."

While the scent of cooking filled the house Galton and the Walk-Man talked.

"Burrowes hasn't asked you to marry his daughter yet?"

"What? No. Why?"

"He asks every lodger. Funny you don't know. It's common knowledge round here."

"You mean," said Galton, showing great interest in the Walk-Man's enquiry, "he wants to marry Gemma off?"

"Yes. Everybody knows. . . . I mean, that house's always got a lodger—and it's always a man. Oh, he doesn't have to be young. Burrowes doesn't care who takes her off his hands. You know what he once called her? 'An embarrassment.' He's a fool, because without her his friends would eat him out. You see all those so-called friends in the shop? As soon as his back's turned they open his beer and pretend they've paid for it. Those are the people he calls friends. But me, the first opportunity he gets he humiliates me. Talk about being vindictive! Once at the shop I made a joke about his lodgers and he never forgave me. Mind you, we're like chalk and cheese; and add to that that I know about his little game with the lodgers."

Galton eyed the Walk-Man suspiciously. He had been in his house less than ten minutes and had already come by information damaging to Burrowes.

"Anyway," pursued the Walk-Man, "*she* won't marry you even if you asked."

"How do you know?" said Galton promptly.

"How do I know? That's my speciality, studying people."

The sound of pounding came from the kitchen.

"She's getting the foo-foo ready," confided the Walk-Man. "You like foo-foo?"

"Yes," answered Galton. "You think you can understand people just by observing them? That's nonsense. Nonsense!"

"Don't get carried away," said the Walk-Man with a look of surprise. "If you want we'll drop the subject."

"I never get carried away," replied Galton coldly.

"Good. I'll continue discussing it with you if you swear you're not sweet on Gemma."

"What? Who said I'm sweet—"

"Come on! You've been seen on the river."

"It's better not to discuss it," Galton remarked curtly.

The Walk-Man's wife came in with a jug of drink.

"I hope Mr . . . ah. I forget. . . ."

"Flood," said Galton.

"I hope you like swank, Mr Flood. This is a teetotaller house."

Had it not been for the Walk-Man's wife and the food being prepared Galton would have gone home. He felt certain that the fright he received earlier on, on catching sight of her, was connected with the self-indulgence of his life at Wismar. His guilt at the pleasure he found in Gemma's company, never far from the surface, had taken the form of the woman's fancied resemblance to his mother. The incident, followed so closely by the disclosures about Mr Burrowes, made him sick at heart, and with each word the Walk-Man spoke withered one of those flowers gathered in Gemma's company in the course of the last few days.

The meal was an ordeal for Galton, but the thought of going back to Mr Burrowes's house, of facing Gemma, now somehow tarnished by the Walk-Man's innuendoes, was equally unpleasant.

"You've lived here long?" Galton asked the good woman.

She told him about the house and their children; and the Walk-Man, cowed by his wife's presence, seemed completely absorbed in his meal. After every few mouthfuls he drank from his cup of swank. When his plate was finally empty he poured another cup from the mug in which a lump of ice floated, flanked by the lime seeds the hostess had neglected to remove.

After the meal the two men were alone once more. The Walk-Man sensed that Galton was no longer interested in what he had to say and was content to sit with him by the window. He had brought the young man home to dazzle him with his talk, but like a firework that fails to go off and lies spluttering in the grass, he only ventured the odd remark about matters of little consequence.

When Galton bade the couple goodbye he eagerly stepped out into the street, empty except for two youths loitering at the corner. The river was deserted and Galton had to wait some time for a boat from Wismar, which landed a young woman carrying a potted bougainvillea.

On the other side he lingered by the wharf, not wishing to go home yet. However, fearing that the inhabitants of the houses which looked on to the river might be watching, he reluctantly made his way to Mr Burrowes's house.

Galton went up by the back stairs and once in his room lay down on his bed. The stillness was broken only by Gemma turning the pages of a book in the adjoining room. Probably, he thought, her father had told her of his invitation to dine with the Walk-Man, so that she did not bother to call out to offer him anything.

He went over the events of the evening, beginning with his visit to the shop, and once again felt deeply hurt at the Walk-Man's opinion that he had been offered the room as a bait to snare him. But what had Burrowes's intentions to do with Gemma's feelings? Galton cursed his own vulnerability. All the happiness he had accumulated these last few weeks was erased with a few words spoken by someone who evidently bore Burrowes a grudge. Yet, even if the Walk-Man had lied he could not live in that house any longer than was necessary.

Was he then so easily offended? He had poisoned the Walk-Man's conversation and eaten at his table without smiling. He envied the laughter of the customers in the shop, their lack of constraint and their ingenuousness.

But, despite the reflections on his own shortcomings Galton saw Gemma and her father as plotters against his liberty; and the Walk-Man's opinion that Gemma would not marry him, even if he asked her, could not shake him in this conviction.

"Who's it?" Galton asked.

"Can I come in?" Gemma's voice came from the other side of the door.

Galton jumped up from the bed. "Come in!"

"You're sure?" she asked, when she had opened the door and looked inside.

"Yes, yes. Come in."

For more than a minute neither spoke. Finally Gemma sat down on the bed, as much at home in his silence as with his words. Galton could find nothing to say.

"You're sick, ne?" she asked.

"No. I've had a disappointment, that's all."

"Ah. . . . You're keeping it to yourself . . . like everything else."

He eyed her as he would a stranger. Not once had his thoughts about her turned to intimacy.

"Inside," said Gemma, "inside, you can read me like a book. But you. . . ."

"Th! That's what *you* say. I don't know anything about you. What d'you see in me for instance? I hate deceit!"

"Ah. . . . You think I'm deceitful?" she asked; and he was unable to understand how she could remain so calm during a conversation which caused him such pain.

"You think I'm deceitful?" she repeated.

"Can you rely on any woman? No, seriously. Can any man rely on a woman?"

The room was dark except for islands of light on the wall above Galton's bed; and occasionally a lamp in the neighbouring range, turned off or on, brought changes to the fractured patterns.

"I can ask you the same question. Can a woman rely on a man? Why should people torture themselves about questions like that? Don't I rely on you? But I never wondered about. . . ."

Galton took a deep breath. "You don't depend on anybody," he said. "Least of all me."

"Oh," she whispered, "you're not always so brutal."

"Am I more brutal than the other lodgers?"

"What other lodgers?" she asked, losing her composure. "People come and go and what's that got to do with me?"

"I'm going away too," Galton said, in an effort to make her suffer.

When Gemma rose from the bed Galton wondered what he could do to restrain her from going. At the same time his pride would not allow him to ask her to remain.

Gemma stopped at the door.

"You don't have to run from me," she said.

"I'm not running!" burst out Galton with unexpected violence.

Gemma closed the door quietly behind her and it seemed to Galton as though he was stranded in some vast, unknown country, without money or resources.

In the dark room, hung with ancient wallpaper, now so familiar to him, an absurd idea filled his mind: he must somehow lick the wall bare of its flowers. On the cover of the book he found open on the dining-table the day before she had written the quotation:

When care draws near
The garden of the soul lies waste.

"Flowers on a partition!" he exclaimed to himself. "Why not put manure while they're at it? Ha! Then they'd see a real garden, where rats hide and come out to devour the flowers at night."

He began wringing his hands in great excitement and muttering to himself; and then, as if responding to some inner prompting, jumped on the bed and began licking the walls in an attempt to remove the flowers. But when his efforts proved vain he was taken with a violent inclination to smash down the door that connected his room to Gemma's.

The piercing signal from a departing bauxite ship was followed by the sound of the front door being closed and Mr Burrowes's voice humming a tune.

"Gemma!" he called out.

She must have gone out to meet him for he began to talk to her in that muted, intimate manner Galton found so irritating.

Only yesterday they had gone walking across the mounds, she and he. He was hoping to take her hands again—as he had done in the boat—but though she kept near to him and her lips were full of laughter he had not dared. They talked of the books he had read and Gemma was impressed by his predilection for authors whose names she had never heard before. She called him "an intellect" and he, flattered by her admiration, confessed to having written his friend Winston about her.

Comforted by these reflections Galton's anger subsided. But he knew that he was unable to remain under Mr Burrowes's roof any longer and resolved to look up the Walk-Man in order to ask him for help in seeking work in the bush. At the same time he secretly hoped for confirmation from the latter of Gemma's innocence.

The following day, the Walk-Man, no doubt remembering Galton's conduct at his table, received him coolly at first.

"I'm sorry about yesterday."

"That's over and done with," the Walk-Man said. "You're not the laughing type anyway."

Galton told him why he had come to Linden and the Walk-Man in turn confided in him, claiming that he and his brother had been robbed of their patrimony by a dishonest lawyer. Neither of them had realised their ambitions to become professional men.

As their conversation progressed Galton found it more and more difficult to ask him for help in finding a job. "It would look as if I only came for that," Galton thought.

"Nice of you to apologise," observed the Walk-Man, now as expansive as ever.

"Fact is," said Galton, "I came about help with a job."

"A job? You?"

"I should've told you as soon as I came," Galton excused himself.

"No. I mean, I don't know. . . . What sort of job?"

"Anything in the bush."

"I can't help you with that; but you can go and see Wilfred. He used to work in the bush. I'll tell you where to find him. . . . All right? What's wrong?"

"Look," said Galton. "If I ask you something you won't laugh? You'll treat it in strict confidence?"

"Sure, sure. What's it?"

"It's about Gemma, Mr. Burrowes's daughter. Do you think she's had anything to do with any lodger?"

"Yesterday I talked like a woman," the Walk-Man answered. "When you left I said to myself, 'He must despise me!' I understand why you were like that at table. And I lied about Burrowes. I can't help it. I like it, you see; I enjoy lying. But afterwards there's a kind of reaction. I vomit whenever I drink. That's why the wife won't allow alcohol in the house. Well, it's the same with lying: I lie, and afterwards, when the satisfaction wears away. . . . Living up here, surrounded by philistines, you develop a mania. The man next door collects butterflies. Butterflies! A grown man. Well, I tell lies."

"You don't have to explain," Galton said eagerly. "God! It's like a weight off my mind. You mean he didn't have lodgers just to marry off Gemma?"

"No! He always had lodgers. It started in the days before the shop when he lost his job."

"So you made the whole thing up!" Galton exclaimed.

"Completely! Now, you see, I've had my satisfaction *and* my forgiveness. I mean, you forgive me, don't you?"

"Of course," Galton said.

"You're not . . . I know you're not running away," said the Walk-Man. "I only said that to dazzle the others. You know what it's like if I'd said I couldn't read your character; they'd have said I was a fake. It's like going to the doctor. If he can't diagnose your sickness you'd think he wasn't any good; so he's got to lie. When all is said and done only children tell the truth."

"What?" asked Galton, stung by his words. "I don't lie."

"Oh," said the Walk-Man, faltering.

Galton looked him up and down contemptuously. Then suddenly recalling his conduct at table the previous day and his remorse afterwards, he smiled.

"My friends—people who know me," observed Galton. "say I take differences of opinion too seriously. I suppose I do."

"My wife says the same of me. In truth! You ask her when she comes in."

The Walk-Man sat down and drew his chair up to Galton's. "My wife's a fantastic woman. She married me to save me from the bottle. And she did! At what cost! She's got the children watching me to see I don't backslide. Imagine putting children to watch their own father."

The Walk-Man laughed unexpectedly and Galton had the impression that he would not have his wife behave otherwise. His words were like froth. If only he had not involved Gemma and her father in his improvisations, Galton thought, it would have been a simple matter to remain at Wismar, look for a job and even marry her. For the doubts raised by his careless talk lingered like the taste of aloes, to spoil an appetite he had longed to assuage.

Galton regretted having confided in him why he had come to Linden. He had not even told Gemma. It was so stupid to confide in a stranger simply because he was nice to you. Surprised and glad that the Walk-Man bore him no grudge with regard to the day before, he had got carried away.

"Don't repeat what I told you about coming to Linden," Galton said.

"Me? I wouldn't tell my own mother."

"What about the job?" he asked, ready to take his leave.

"Wait, I'll write Wilfred's address on a piece of paper." The Walk-Man fumbled in his pocket for a pencil. In the end he went inside and came back with a neatly folded piece of paper which Galton took and opened.

"It's about ten houses up on the other side of the road. Tell him I sent you."

Galton could hear the Walk-Man humming behind him and thought of Mr Burrowes and the manner in which he looked on during the character reading session. It seemed to him that his interest in the proceedings had been unusually keen.

Hardly had Galton gone a few yards down the road than he met the Walk-Man's wife.

"Eh, Mr Flood, you coming from our house?"

"Yes. I went to see your husband."

"He been expecting you."

"Me? I didn't tell him I was coming today," observed Galton.

"He been looking out of the window all the time and I had to ask him if he got ants in he pants. And he say he waiting for you. This was early in the morning."

"I definitely didn't say I was coming," Galton said, wondering if he had in fact promised to come.

"Well, he say so. I think he wanted to see you so bad he was hoping."

She lowered her head and Galton pretended to be looking back at the house.

"He's always quarrelling," she said. "And when anyone don't agree with him—oh, me Lord! You would think they do him something bad. . . . But as I say, he been sitting on eggs all morning, waiting for you. . . . I got to be going then."

"Goodbye," Galton replied.

"Wait, ne. You going come to see him again, eh? At least you can come on Sunday when the children home. They always gallivanting somewhere in the week as if they only got a week to live."

"All right. When I see him again," Galton promised.

He hurried away, hoping to find Wilfred home.

FOUR

Two years later Galton was standing beside the Chai-Chai airstrip in the upper Mazaruni River. Having placed his hold-all on the ground, he waited for the pilot to give the signal for him and the six other passengers to board the plane, but the pilot, standing a few yards away, was haggling with an Amerindian over the purchase of a bird which was fluttering helplessly in an oval cage. On each occasion that he named a price lower than the one quoted by the Amerindian the latter referred him to his wife.

"Ask she, ne?"

The pilot would then look at the woman who, shaking her head stubbornly, stood by the original quotation.

"All right, three dollars," he suggested, with a note of finality in his voice as he edged nearer to the five dollars first quoted.

"Ask she, ne?" reiterated the Amerindian, turning to his wife. But she again shook her head.

"Can it sing?" asked the pilot.

"Yes," declared the man.

"What's he eat?"

"Anything," said the woman.

In the end they agreed on a price of four dollars.

While the passengers were boarding the plane Galton, on an impulse, asked the pilot: "You're selling it? I'll give you eight dollars."

"Take it," the latter said after hesitating.

Galton paid him and took the cage. The idea had occurred to him that it would make a suitable present for his brother Selwyn. The bird was a tawa-tawa, one of the best songsters in the country.

The pilot fastened his seat belt and the others did the same. Galton, noticing that the Amerindian sitting next to him could not secure his, leaned over and attached it for him. The man grinned and confessed that it was the first time that he was travelling.

The ten-seater plane advanced slowly between the staves that had been recently placed along the whole length of the strip, turned and taxied to the top, where it swerved and came to a halt. Then, with a roar, it started off again, gathering speed swiftly. Suddenly, Galton was aware that they were above the trees.

Soon, after the initial curiosity as to what was outside had passed, most of the passengers either fell asleep or leaned back in their seats. The sun was high up and it was uncomfortably close in the plane. Galton, who kept staring out of the window, was soon lost in his reflections.

The first few weeks in the bush he had enjoyed the aloneness, the silent river and above all his job as a diver. When he had had enough he would exchange with one of the men and work on the raft. Once the pumping was over, the excitement of lifting out the rectangular sections that held the gravel, of shovelling it into the metal container through the three sieves, and finally of examining it for diamonds, was invariably the same as the first time.

The men he worked with liked him, though they found him withdrawn. When they sat around the charcoal fire telling stories at night, Galton listened attentively, but never contributed any of his own. He laughed at their ribaldry, regretting not having the same experience with women some of them claimed to have.

On Sundays he and John, an Amerindian who kept them supplied with cassava bread, often went up-river in a canoe fashioned from purple heart bark, a frail craft that made its way effortlessly through the glass-smooth brown water. Here, in the upper reaches of the Mazaruni, the fish were small, as John had warned Galton; but he was to learn that it was so, after several fruitless attempts to catch anything worthwhile. The two men sometimes brought down a duck with their rusty guns or shot a labba. As a rule, however, they just paddled close to the banks or visited John's garden place in the jungle, where he grew cassava and bananas, or sat smoking by the river under the tall mahogany trees. About an hour after dusk, a pervasive silence would settle over the jungle, broken only by the sharp cry of some animal falling victim to a larger predator. He and John used to sit for hours without saying a word to each other. Then some trivial incident might cause John to burst out laughing; as when Galton got up to urinate against a tree or dropped the tobacco from the paper in which he was rolling a cigarette.

But Galton discovered that for him the presence of a woman was essential and could see no alternative to going back to Georgetown. He put off his decision as long as he could, unwilling to give up the camaraderie and his hammock under the tarpaulin, where at nights he delivered himself up to recollections of his father, with whom he had occasionally spent whole afternoons fishing or exploring the back dams.

After he had given in his notice he wondered if he had done the right thing. Might it not be better to bring a wife out into the interior, build his own hut and raise his children in the freedom of the bush? Anyway, his mind was made up.

The last afternoon, as he sat eating his cassava bread and drinking coffee from his enamel cup, one of the men remarked, "You gwine get married, eh?"

"No, not yet," Galton rejoined.

"Ha! He got a woman line up in Georgetown. I bet he send she the money for she satin dress and all. I bet you!" another one of his workmates exclaimed.

"You don't play cards; you don't drink; you don't talk 'bout wife. Is what you going do in you spare time, then? Fuck the dogs, as the Yankee man them does say?"

This remark was greeted with a guffaw. Galton did not mind.

"Hi, boss man!" the first man addressed their employer, "Wha' 'bout some beef tonight, eh? We going miss this great big silence next to we." He nodded in Galton's direction, got up and stretched himself.

That night Galton drank raw rum to please the men and fetched out a ribald story from the corners of his memory. John recounted how he once found a porknocker in the jungle, his face ravaged by a bushmaster, which must have attacked him in a frenzy. He went on to acquaint them with the lore of the bushmaster.

"Even if you get the man to hospital right away and save he life, the place where he get bite, say he hand, going to wither away," John declared.

"Why?" asked one of the men.

"'Cause that particular snake paison does attack the nerves. Even labaria paison don't do that. But bushmaster is another business."

And so the men spent the first half of the night, passing the rum bottle, telling stories and listening to John speak of the Ackawaio Indians, their origins and their lore. When they took to their hammocks Galton was unable to fall asleep.

Selwyn had married soon after he came out into the bush and now had a six-month-old baby. How would he take to the idea of his brother coming to live with him and his wife? What was she like?

"Tch!" thought Galton. "The house is mine as much as his. I didn't say anything when his new wife moved into it."

Nevertheless he was unable to shake off the doubts. Invariably, he used to drop off before the nights became uncomfortably cold, but now the chill air seeped through the gaps in his hammock, causing him to shiver and toss. He got up, placed a log of dry wood across the smouldering pile and climbed back into his hammock.

The next morning he was awakened by the chug-chugging of the pump sucking up gravel from the river bed. He felt left out and more certain than ever that he had been hasty in giving up the job.

When he waved goodbye to the others and stepped into a boat to which John had attached an outboard motor he heard one of the men shout, "Duck!" A pair of ducks winged past, nervously skimming the water. A few hundred yards on the boat caught up with the wild ducks, which had settled on the river, close to the opposite bank. They both took off once more, following the river where it curved in the distance.

On arriving at the airstrip Galton found the plane waiting and the other passengers chatting in groups. And then, from the opposite direction, the Amerindian couple arrived with their oval bird cage.

John, shading his eyes from the sun, impassively informed Galton that it would rain later that day. With that he turned and left him standing beside his hold-all.

FIVE

Two cars were put at the disposal of the passengers after they had landed at Ogle late in the afternoon. The noise of traffic on the East Coast road contrasted with the sounds that preceded the silence in the jungle at sunset. The car in which he was riding overtook two dray-carts and accelerated gradually until it was exceeding the speed limit. Galton lowered the window to let in the sea breeze, which smothered his face and ruffled everything.

It was Easter Monday and the sky over the sea wall was dotted with coloured kites. The car turned into Sherrif Street along which groups of children, accompanied by their parents, were returning from an afternoon of kite flying. When the vehicle stopped at the head of David Street Galton got out and dragged his hold-all after him.

A few minutes later he paused on the bridge before the house which had been his home since he was a boy. The tall, pillarlike cabbage palm that soared above the roof had grown alarmingly and now exceeded the height of the house by at least fifteen feet.

"Galton!"

Selwyn had put his head through one of the windows, unnoticed by his brother.

"What you standing there for?" Selwyn asked him.

Galton's fears about the kind of welcome he would receive were allayed by his brother's greeting. He raised the iron latch that secured the gate and mounted the stairs to the porch, where Selwyn had come out to meet him.

"The dog must've remembered you; he didn't bark," Selwyn said, grinning broadly.

Galton followed his brother inside and at once caught sight of a young woman who was carrying an infant on her arm.

"Come, ne?" Selwyn urged his wife. "This is Galton. Come on, I tell you. Shake his hand."

Nekka stretched out her free hand, staring at him, expressionless.

"Don't bother to say the baby look like me," said Selwyn. "I'm worried that everybody saying it. . . ."

He was interrupted by his wife. "Y'know I don't like that sort of joke."

"All right, all right! She takes everything seriously," said Selwyn. Then, turning to his wife he said, "Give me Sonny and hot up some food for Galton."

Selwyn took the baby into the gallery, where his brother followed him.

"You don't want the bird I brought you?" Galton asked.

"For me? Nekka! We got a bird."

Then, to Galton, he observed: "I've never seen a cage like this, man. Where you pick it up?"

He put the baby down on the floor and submitted the cage to a close examination.

Galton's resentment at the possibility that he might feel a stranger in his own home was deepened by his sister-in-law's cool attitude.

"How you liked it in the bush?" asked Selwyn. "Just suit you, eh?"

Galton had sat down in the Berbice chair opposite him. Instead of answering his brother's question, he asked, "You're sure she doesn't mind?"

Selwyn had picked up the baby once more.

"Mind? Is your house as much as mine."

"Don't give me that," Galton rejoined testily. "You're always like that. I want to know if *she* minds, not *you*."

"I tell you, no," Selwyn reassured him. "You haven't changed. You're still so damn suspicious."

Galton was ashamed.

"It's not that. Tch!" he exclaimed. "You've got a wife and child. When all is said and done, in her place. . . ."

"Since I tell you is all right!" Selwyn said impatiently.

He began to talk about the neighbours. The youngest boy was at university. But soon Galton was no longer listening. His mind went back to his home in the jungle and he recalled the first day he picked wild jamoon. That morning he ate so many his hands were stained a deep purple.

"Since you've been away," said Selwyn, "they've built the estate at Peter's Hall, where your friend Winston was going to live. He's been round here looking for you."

"I told him I was going," rejoined Galton.

"Anyway, he's gone and got married."

"Winston?"

The bit of news seemed to disturb Galton, who looked at his brother in surprise.

"What about Jessie?" Galton enquired.

"Is Jessie he married," Selwyn replied.

"Oh," Galton said, relieved.

Selwyn went on talking, as if it was he who had been away. Occasionally, when the infant showed signs of restlessness, he tapped its back with his left hand.

"It ready!" Nekka called out, and the two men got up and went into the dining-room where Selwyn handed over the sleeping child to his wife, who adjusted it on her arms and muttered soft sounds to comfort it.

Selwyn watched his brother eating.

"Listen," he said, as if he had just remembered something he ought to have mentioned before. "Nekka and I agreed that you won't have to pay us for food, since you own half the house. It's like rent we ought to be paying you. See? When you start working you can give her a couple of dollars a week for sheets, soap and so on. What you think of that?"

"Sounds fair to me," said Galton, glad that the matter had been settled so quickly.

"Tell him 'bout the letter, ne?" Nekka said to her husband, behind whom she was standing.

"Oh, yes, I forgot!" Selwyn exclaimed, striking his forehead. "There's a letter for you. From the scent and all it must be a woman."

"A woman?"

Selwyn went inside and fetched the letter. Galton waited until the meal was over and when he was alone in the gallery tore it open. It was from Gemma and was dated nine months previously. But why had Selwyn not sent it to Chai-Chai?

"Of course!" Galton thought to himself, remembering that his brother only got to know his address when he had written two weeks before that he was coming home.

The letter ran:

My dear tormentor,

We moved to McKenzie, but then moved back across the river to Wismar last year. Nearly all the men have gone away and those that remain, well. I don't have to describe them, do I? I love you. I know you wouldn't come and live here, so far away from your beloved Georgetown, but if you send for me I will fly to you like an impatient bird. Father says it's not you I love, only an idea. What's the difference? I asked him. But the matter was too important for me to argue with him about it. He says that any man, however ugly, who had stayed in our house at the time you did would have made an impression on me. Sometimes he is so vulgar!

I read all day and night and spend the rest of the time thinking of what marriage might be like. Don't write me, it would spoil everything. I want to suffer on your account and can imagine nothing so boring as constant happiness. (Of course, write if you want me to come to you.)

Today we had the orange tree in the yard cut down and collected the few fruit on it. I still have the taste of bitter oranges in my mouth.

I long to write you so much, but when I pick up my pen I don't know what I want to say. I would really like to write you about ten letters at ten sittings so that I could get down all the things I want to tell you, as they come to my simple mind. For me you are still the Great Intellect who came and went, like some wilful gust of wind.

Goodbye, my Tormentor,

Gemma

P.S. Another thing Father says is that you went away because the Walk-Man filled you up with a lot of lies about him. I told him you were not like that. They were good friends, you know, but they quarrelled a few years ago.

Gemma

Galton wished fervently that no one would interrupt him for a while. So she remembered! Send for her? Of course he would send for her! As soon as he got a job he would send for her and they would get married. He could not do what his friend Winston had done for years; he could not live with a woman in sin.

"She writes like all those books she reads," he thought.

Galton recalled the time, when as a schoolboy, he read every novel he could put his hands on. But the phase had passed. He wondered if her father still ran the shop in the arcade, with its coloured electric bulbs and pictures cut out from American magazines. What if he went and settled at Wismar, with the money he had saved in the bush? But he rejected the thought almost at once. Was she right about his unwillingness to leave Georgetown? Whenever he was here he thought of going away, but once in some other place he felt its irresistible pull.

That night Galton fell asleep thinking of Gemma, and dreamed of his dead father, who spoke in a way he could not understand. Then his father became John, his Amerindian friend, behind whom he was sitting in a corial. John was paddling in his unhurried style, close to the bank of a black-water creek. Ahead of them was a swarm of morpho butterflies, and those that had alighted on an overhanging branch were opening and closing their wings in leisurely fashion. He awoke to hear the dog barking and, sitting up, wondered for a while where he was. When he lay down again he thought how absurd it was that a man should have a room to himself. In the bush the dark outlines of bulging hammocks kept you company when you were awake and strange forms came up from the river to dissolve a few feet away from the tarpaulin.

"Why do I never dream of my mother?" he thought, brooding over the idea for some time.

Even though his mother had not died so long ago he was unable to fix his thoughts on her for long.

The longing for Gemma unsettled him. And yet he finally had to admit that he did not want to get married, not ever. At the time of his stay in Linden he believed that he was too young to "get hooked"; now, at twenty-four, with twelve hundred dollars in his pocket, his reasons for remaining single seemed less convincing. If he desired so passionately to stay in Georgetown he and Gemma could set up shop here, away from her father, whom Galton saw as the most serious impediment to his union with her.

"A man's greatest gifts are a deep sleep and a good woman," Winston, his best friend, liked to say when he was drunk. Galton now rarely slept well, but at least he had found a good woman, who remembered him after all this time.

"When you find her don't hesitate! Grab her and rush to the altar at high speed!" Winston once said, echoing his own father's sentiments.

But Winston, despite his advice, had lived with his woman for years before marrying her. She had fathered his girl child and demonstrated her love for him in a way that had won their friends' admiration. Nevertheless, Winston was honest and loved him as his father had. When Galton wrote him about Gemma he advised him to marry her. All the signs were propitious, he had urged.

Galton reviewed the relations between the married couples he knew. They all seemed satisfactory; and Winston and Jessie especially, whom he had known for years, were particularly happy. Well, he must get a job as soon as he could, then face the problem squarely.

If only he could sleep through one night! In the jungle the shadows sometimes kept him awake, while in town it was the dogs that woke him up. They roamed everywhere, making the long nights their own. No one else seemed to be disturbed by them, least of all Selwyn, who never once complained of being unable to sleep. Yet they were there, with their luminous eyes and dripping mouths, padding through the grey silence of the night, disturbing the quiet with petulant outbreaks of barking.

SIX

Galton dropped off two hours before sunrise, and when he woke up he found that the family had breakfasted hours ago and that Selwyn had gone to work. He saw Nekka in the kitchen with the maid, and the baby dawdling on the floor, naked. It was only then Galton noticed that the infant was a boy. He was examining his body with great interest, accompanying his discoveries with squeals and fatuous smiles.

"Your breakfast's on the table," Nekka declared, on catching sight of him. She smiled as she spoke and appeared to be more genial than when he arrived the night before.

"You sleep good?" she asked.

Before he could answer she was undoing the flask with which Galton was having some difficulty.

"The letter was bad news yesterday, eh?" she asked.

"No, why?"

"Nothing. You din' look the same when you did finish reading it."

The maid, a middle-aged woman, came into the dining-room to take some utensil from the cupboard over the refrigerator. She smiled weakly at Galton, who noticed a pile of okroes and bolonjays on the draining-board, where she had been standing. He could not, the first day he was back, inform them that he did not eat okroes. There were other things, little things, but important to him. Would his sister-in-law ever understand?

Breakfast over, he set out at once to look for work. That night Selwyn was astounded to hear that his brother had accepted a job as a watchman in a sawmill in Lower Water Street.

"How much you're getting?" he asked Galton.

"Twenty-two fifty a week," Galton replied, not flinching before Selwyn's half-mocking, half-puzzled gaze.

Galton's brother stopped eating and placed his knife and fork on the table, where the family were sitting at their evening meal.

"You must be mad! You been in the bush too long, that's it. Let's face it, you must be mad!"

"Don't . . ." Galton began.

"For Christ's sake! Working in a sawmill! As a watchman? Is that what you got an education for? To sit at night in front of a pile of wood watching the stray dogs copulate? Well, I ask you! What was the use of your education?"

Selwyn got up angrily and turned his back on his wife and his brother.

"I'm starting on Monday and you might as well accept it," observed Galton dryly.

The brothers did not speak to each other for two days, until Selwyn recounted an incident that had occurred in his drug store. Galton shared his amusement and Nekka noticed how Selwyn's laughter was deep and how the words came hurriedly. She smiled inwardly at his weakness and his loyalty. In the end, Galton's decision was to be respected and he would never again voice his objection.

The fact was that Galton made no effort to look for work in keeping with his qualifications and Selwyn and Nekka spoke of little else in bed.

"He'll never be able to marry with a job like that," he remarked to his wife one night.

"Probably he don't want to get married. They got a lot of men like that," Nekka rejoined.

"Since he's been in the bush something happened to him. It's as if he doesn't care. I wonder if. . . ."

"He know this woman in Wismar good?" she asked Selwyn, who looked at her without answering.

"Wha' wrong?" she asked.

"How d'you know where she's living?" he demanded, a suspicious note in his voice.

"The letter stamp Wismar," Nekka replied without hesitation.

"How you see the letter?" he pursued.

"It on the table in his room!" she exclaimed. "What you staring at me for?"

"You've been reading his letter!" he accused her.

"I didn't read his letter!" she burst out angrily.

"Liar!"

Selwyn continued to accuse her and she persisted in her denial that she had not read his brother's letter.

When Galton returned home the lights were out. The dog wagged its tail, but remained under the house, its front legs stretched out to form a resting place for its head. Galton sat down on the topmost step, for he was in no hurry to go to bed. On the waste ground opposite, the Baptist school, with its elongated windows, squatted among the shadows of the silk cotton and Christmas trees.

Galton was considering the possibility of leaving his brother's house and going to live with Winston. His friend had offered him the accommodation that very night at a rent somewhat below the market price. It was to his advantage, Winston claimed, to have some man on the premises during the day, when he was out at work. Yesterday Galton would have declined the offer without more, but the discovery that his letter had been tampered with incensed him. It had evidently been hastily replaced in the envelope and he came to the conclusion that Nekka was in the act of reading it when he returned home that afternoon. A long time ago, between himself and his brother, there had been established limits to the space they considered to be theirs. Above all, neither ever went into the other's room, so that each was in the habit of leaving personal belongings about, knowing that they would not be disturbed.

The consequences of attempting to initiate Nekka into this ritualistic behaviour could not be foreseen; yet if Selwyn, obliged to share with her, could hardly hope to preserve his independence, he, Galton, on the other hand, did not have to tolerate such an encroachment on his private space. He would mention the incident to Selwyn. But why should he cause his brother unnecessary suffering? It was best to go away, leaving their mutual goodwill intact.

Galton dared not admit to himself that he was distressed, less by Nekka's officiousness than by the affluence of his brother's household.

The next night he was to begin working and when at six o'clock he presented himself at the sawmill he had already changed his mind about moving out.

The premises reeked of the sweet scent of new lumber, piled in planks on both sides of the entrance. At the back, under an adjoining shed, much higher than the one that led on to the pavement, were huge mounds of wood of all kinds: purpleheart, more wallaba, silver balli and the yellow, indestructible greenheart. The sawmill on the eastern side of the street was lit up by the soft rays of the sinking sun. That portion of Water Street which stretched from Stabroek Market southwards was almost unknown to most Georgetonians, who believed that the road terminated at the market. It was an area of sawmills and timber yards and one metal workshop, silent and indolent, where, in the daytime the watchmen sat dreaming or lay on long rugs beside the narrow gutters. At night, the only sign of life was the noises from Lombard Street with its alleyways and mysterious recesses. This was the world in which Galton chose to work, where his most active moments would be devoted to checking the timber delivered by barge at a wharf on the opposite side of the road, or comparing a lorry driver's invoice against the boards on his vehicle.

The old watchman whom Galton was relieving reviewed his duties briskly, not making any secret of his desire to get away home.

"Night is the best; hardly nothing does ever come. And if they ketch you asleeping y'can always say y'been praying. They like religious people."

When Galton asked him to explain something he rejoined, "A educated man like you so tchupid!" and tossed his head impatiently.

"You sure you in' a spy?" the watchman enquired, just before leaving. "You in' no watchman."

At first, the lack of routine, the overpowering scent of wood were too much for him, but within a few weeks he had become accustomed to it. He took advantage of the empty hours to follow a correspondence course in radio technology and spent the little money he had left over on bits of electronic equipment.

One night when he was disinclined to concentrate on the content of his latest course work he wrote to Gemma.

Dear Gemma

As you suggested, I did not bother to write although, in fact, I wanted to.

First of all I must tell you that I got a job as a watchman and earn twenty-two fifty a week. This is not what I want to do, but it gives me a lot of time to work at a radio course I took up a couple of weeks ago—by way of insurance for the future.

I can't really say what I think of your letter. At first I believed it was one big pretence, but then it might really be a side of you I don't know. You seem to know exactly what you want. Not me. If you realised how uncertain I was about everything you would lose all faith in me.

I am very happy living with my brother and sister-in-law. She is attentive and makes me feel guilty about the way I treated her in the beginning.

Little by little I am losing spiritual contact with the jungle. The first week I could not bear the noise the dogs made at night and the cocks crowing at morning. That's all past now.

There is a big family living next door. I believe I told you about them when I was in Linden. They are all mad! Selwyn says that one of the girls likes me (there are seven of them), but she never takes any notice of me, at least as far as I can see. In fact I would say she is completely indifferent to me.

Write me a long letter.

Affectionately,
Galton

The reply came three days later.

Dear Galton,

You are the most devious, the most insensitive person I know. Up to the day your letter arrived I was at peace with myself. In fact I had almost forgotten you existed. Now you've made me mad with jealousy. Tell me something, Galton: Do you really think I am interested in the women who are supposed to like you, or your fantasies about them? I don't know how old these seven females living next door to you are, but I am supremely indifferent to their behaviour towards you.

You deliberately took a menial job so that you might have an excuse for not marrying me. Can't you understand I love you? The women I know never really loved a man. When I hear them talk I see that they only hanker after marriage. Of course I want to marry you, but not in the same way they want to get married. I loathe you because you are so weak and frightened. Suppose we got married and did not get on and we separated, would that be the end of the world? You think I would demean myself by dragging you in front of a divorce court? If you were not then man enough to support any children of our marriage I would fly as far away from you as possible. Oh, Galton, you have killed something in me that can never be revived.

Do you remember the mountains of bauxite waste at Wismar, where we used to go walking? Those Sundays when we left the streets and walked up and up, and then looked down at the blue-green water between the mounds. When your letter came I deliberately tortured myself by leaving it on the dining-table. Pa asked me what was in it—he recognised your handwriting—and I told him he would have to wait. After all, I was waiting. You men lock women up in small places and expect them to be normal. These fires burning inside me are not normal. My dreams aren't normal; the way I walk isn't normal. If I were normal I would open the window and scream until something burst. There is an East Indian girl living here who did that a little while ago. Her parents sent for the pharmacist, who gave her some medicine and a sedative. Like all men he believes there must be a medicine for every condition. I and many women like me could tell that she couldn't take it any more, her parents, the music in the streets at night, the sounds from the dance hall down the road, the short skirts she was forbidden to wear and a hundred and one little things.

Knowing you, you won't be able to make head or tail of this letter. Very well, my tormentor. I forgive you. It might be better we never saw each other any more, because, if you touched me I might stop loving you.

Father isn't well. He asked me to give you his regards and ask you to come and see us when you can.

I can see, through the window, a bauxite ship moving down the river. In a few hours it will pass your dear Georgetown and sail out to sea. Last week I was reading a description of an aeroplane journey. The author wrote, "Above was the cobalt sky and below the sea, through a veil of clouds." I put down the book and could not stop thinking of the sea. I always imagine land as representing the limits and limitations of life and the sea as death, boundless, timeless.

Have you changed much since I last saw you, my tormentor? Are your shoulders broader, your hands larger and more cruel? Every letter I write you is longer than the last. Father thinks you write well. I don't. Your letter was full of self-pity and bad sentences. "Little by little I am losing spiritual contact with the jungle." I suppose I feel obliged to criticise everything in you that shows an attachment for some thing or person other than me. But that was really a bad sentence.

Once there was a man who had a dog that bit him, out of sheer boredom. He was so surprised and hurt he told his friends about it. One friend advised him to chain the dog; another told him to beat it; and a third said that to guard against the dog attacking him again he must kill it. You know what the man did? He chained the dog, beat it and then killed it. Just to please all of his friends! I don't know why I've told you this story. Just chaining an animal is cruel. After all, that's what we do to one another, don't we? The English demonstrate their passion for dogs by castrating them. "Doctoring" they call it. O my God! One day I'm going to set fire to the house or something. If you don't come to me soon or send for me I won't be responsible for the consequences.

Goodbye, my TORMENTOR.
I detest you!!

P.S. Women need to write letters, Galton. It is a need with deep, deep roots.

Yours for all time,
Gemma

Galton was curiously excited by this letter. He replaced it in its envelope and read the address:

Galton Flood,
David St.,
Kitty,
Greater Georgetown.

His name was suddenly strange to him, as if he had seen it for the first time. The bold handwriting appeared to impart added significance to "Galton." "Galton! Galton!" he imagined her saying, "You are the most devious. . . ."

Though he would have sworn that he had not deliberately taken the job to avoid marrying he felt he could not deny that his letter to her had not been entirely honest. But there was no resentment at being caught out; only shame and a strong desire to make amends. That night while alone on duty he read and re-read the letter, and the conviction that this woman would make him a good wife grew.

SEVEN

Galton was awakened by the quarrelling and looked at the clock beside his bed, which said twenty past twelve. Selwyn must have just come home for lunch. Usually it was his brother's car drawing up outside the house or the conversation at table that woke Galton. He would then get up and dine with them. The night before had been his night off and he had gone to Winston's house, where Jessie's birthday had provided the excuse for a jump-up. It must have been three o'clock in the morning when he returned home, so that Selwyn's arrival had not disturbed his deep sleep.

"He kian' stay for ever and ever. What going happen when the second one born?" he heard Nekka say.

"Keep your voice down, you idiot!" Selwyn enjoined her.

"Don't call me a idiot!" she screamed at him.

"Then stop behaving like one."

"Who the hell you think you family is? I couldn't bring my family here and le' them do what they like. Ha! I would never hear the end of it."

Galton knew how it would end. She would go off and sulk in the gallery and he would come after her and coo into her ear. She would pretend to be inconsolable, but in the end they would kiss each other passionately and start talking in whispers.

When Galton first discovered that his sister-in-law resented his presence he was so hurt he resolved to go. It only fortified his suspicion, first aroused by the incident with the letter, that it was impossible to share a house with her. Apart from her officiousness she was ill-bred and arrogant, often treating her servant with considerable harshness.

But Galton put off his decision to leave and, with time, learned to ignore his sister-in-law's sallies. He often asked himself what his brother saw in her, for there was no doubt as to Selwyn's affection. He followed her with his eyes continually as if he was seeing her for the first time. Galton would have liked him to see Nekka as she really was: coarse. Mrs Bourne, their neighbour, was afraid of her sharp tongue and, on numerous occasions, only avoided quarrelling with her by fleeing upstairs. Galton had to admit to a certain jealousy when he heard his brother enumerating Nekka's virtues to a visitor. He told the story of how she took over the servant's duties without complaining when the latter was ill and could not come to work. Much of what Selwyn was saying was true, which pained Galton all the more. But his brother was blind if he was unable to see what everyone else could.

Galton got up, changed and took a shower. As he stepped out of the bathroom Beth, the servant, asked, "You want you food now?" He nodded and went back to his room, where he shaved over the wash-basin.

"You up?" Selwyn's voice came from the gallery.

"Yes, why?" Galton answered.

"Nothing."

Selwyn could not tell from his brother's voice if he had heard Nekka say, "He kian' stay for ever and ever." He came and joined Galton at table, on which Beth had just put a plate of fried fish, rice and dhalpourri.

"How's business?" Galton asked him.

"Not too good. An Indian started up a drug store down the road. He does open an hour earlier and close an hour later. You can't compete with people like that."

"Do the same then," Galton suggested.

"I must have a social life, man. I'm not a machine."

Galton looked up at his brother. His smooth skin, his clear, untroubled eyes were those of a man who was well looked after. He called to mind Nekka's attentions and reflected that they could not be the genuine expression of a character such as hers. Sooner or later her bad ways would destroy the foundations of her marriage.

"Nekka's expecting again," Selwyn declared.

"Don't you want it?"

"Shh!" Selwyn warned, and nodded in the direction of the gallery.

"I don't mind," he added.

"Oh."

In the silence that followed Galton thought back on the days when they spoke frankly to each other, scorning any ruse or dissembling.

"I'm moving," Galton declared.

Selwyn hesitated, then said, "Because of Nekka?"

"No. I want to get married. Winston's got two free bedrooms and's been on at me for months to live there. He doesn't want to take a stranger in."

"Ah," Selwyn said. He never imagined that the matter could be settled so painlessly. The desire to be completely frank with his brother almost made Galton confess why he was moving out.

As for Selwyn, Nekka's continual nagging, the fact that she was expecting, the constraint on their behaviour imposed by Galton's presence, all made it difficult for him to maintain the view that his brother was entitled to live there because he was part owner of the house and had lived there all his life.

Selwyn's relief at learning of his brother's impending departure caused him, momentarily, to forget to evince some interest in the disclosure that he intended marrying. If only he could be sure Galton had not heard what Nekka said before she began shouting.

The telephone rang and was answered by Nekka, who called out, "Is for you!"

Selwyn got up and left Galton alone at table. The latter's disgust at his brother's indifference was so profound he felt like running out of the house and as far away from it as his legs could take him. When he was a child he often had fantasies about destroying his parents. It was only Selwyn who was constant. He would never have believed that a woman could sway him to the extent of persuading him that it was necessary to put his own brother out of the family house. What difference would another child make? As things were the boy could not be put in a room by himself for some years yet. Galton regretted not having followed his instincts and taken up Winston's offer when it was first made. He had lost his pride and could never again look on Nekka without feelings of hatred.

Selwyn kissed his wife goodbye and left, apparently as a result of the telephone call. When Nekka came to the back of the house Galton went into the gallery, ostensibly to read the newspaper, as he usually did after lunch.

The sun was streaming through a casement window Selwyn must have opened. Galton closed one flap of it, the panes of which were of thick, patterned glass, to reduce the harshness of the sun's rays. He then lay down in the Berbice chair, under the Demerara window. This had been his father's favourite resting spot, but since his death the window had never been opened, and the bolts that anchored its shutters were welded to their stays by a layer of rust.

Unable to bear the stifling heat, Galton got up to open another window and lower the Venetian blind over it. Instead of lying down again in the Berbice chair he stood looking through the laths at the waste land opposite where three sheep were foraging among the dead leaves under the silk cotton trees. He and Selwyn had often played there as boys or tested their home-made kites before hazarding them in the brisker wind of the sea wall.

The cords that regulated the Venetian blinds were dangling in the breeze and their plastic tips made a tapping sound as they came into contact with the wooden window frames.

Everything seemed to come in waves, hatred, fulfilment and even death. From the start there was a certain ebb and flow in his mounting dislike for Nekka, just as there had been a growing and a slackening of everyone's awareness of his mother's impending death. And this longing for Gemma that had to be satisfied, did it not follow a similar pattern, receding from him and submerging him in turn?

Winston had advised him to marry Gemma. He had an instinct for the right solution, even in matters to which he had given little thought. In fact, Gemma had written as much: marry and if things did not work out, separate. It was she who would be at a disadvantage, with the responsibility of bringing up the children of their marriage. But for him marriage meant a union for life, a certainty beforehand that it would not fail. He had not soiled his body in pre-marital associations, only because his guilt would be intolerable, rendering him incapable of exercising that moral authority he associated with the head of a family. Marital obligations were as grave, on the man's side, as on the woman's; in fact more so.

"But if I've prepared myself," he thought, "and the success of my marriage would depend more on me than on my wife, why've I waited?"

The silence in the house, his fear of doing something hasty, caused him to get up and go out. At the gate the milkman was ladling out milk in a pint measure to a group of women who surrounded him. One of them complained that he was several hours late; she was sure that his milk had gone sour. Unperturbed, he was bending down over a two-gallon aluminium can in order to fill the jug Beth had just given him.

"He in' care; he rich already," Beth said.

"I got a cousin; he is a inspector and I going tell he 'bout you and le' he inspect you milk," the neighbour's servant threatened.

"Is that what you husband does do?" the milkman remarked, glancing at her massive bosom. At this the women burst out laughing.

"My husband got no time for that nonsense," said the woman.

"I got a lot a time and I know just what to look for," rejoined the milkman with a straight face.

"You in' shame?" another woman asked. "In front of these two girl chile?"

The two girls, in their early teens, were smiling, not quite certain whether they should join in the general hilarity.

Galton passed them and headed for Vlissingen Road. There he waited for a bus under the trees.

Half an hour later he was standing by the wharf at the head of Water Street, watching a group of five men unload wood from a barge. The sweat dripped from their faces as they passed the logs from one to the other. The last in the line, an old man, was piling them neatly atop a waist-high heap about a yard from the edge of the wharf.

The ebbing tide had left a length of old rope exposed on the mud where, from innumerable holes, tiny crabs were waving their claws continually. Galton sat in the shadow of a shed adjoining the wharf and waited for the sun to go down. Why, after all, had he become a watchman? He had thereby angered his brother, attracted the ridicule of Winston and caused talk amongst the neighbours.

"Mr Flood boy a watchman! Eh, eh! Whoever hear such a thing?" he could imagine the vaudeville artist saying to his sister-in-law.

At the time he had enjoyed the general consternation caused by his choice of work. Today, the perversity of his attitude was so manifest, he wondered how he could have deceived himself all this time. He must find work that earned him sufficient money to support a family.

A strange sense of elation had taken the place of his anger. At work that night he would write Gemma and offer to marry her. No, no. He first had to speak to Winston and confirm that they could live in his house, as he had suggested, for nothing would induce him to set up a home in the same house with his brother's wife.

Galton was tempted to shout out at the men that he was getting married, that he would find another job and leave these damned woodyards. What a gulf there was between one's thoughts and one's behaviour! Especially his! He was so obsessed with boundaries; the boundaries of propriety, of pride, of privacy, of love. And yet he was unable to come to terms with the fact that Selwyn had set boundaries to his affection for him, in the interest of domestic harmony.

"How long's he known Nekka? Two? Three years? We were brothers and at one time inseparable," he thought.

What did he expect of Gemma? There must be no compromise in her love for him; but such a compromise he thought desirable in Selwyn's love for Nekka.

Galton looked at his watch. It was a quarter to six, when the shadows are long. A man, who must have been fishing on the other side of the wharf, approached him, his tackle over his shoulder and three fishes strung through their gills, dangling from his right hand. As he went by he muttered a greeting to Galton, who, lost in thought, was not at first aware that he had been addressed and ignored the man. Suddenly realising what had happened Galton spun round.

"Hi!" he shouted after the man, who turned and smiled so readily that Galton felt as if he had been taken in a shameful act. The stranger went out of sight round the corner, walking slowly.

Then the sun sank and night came suddenly. And the stray dogs emerged from the alleys to wander about in the darkness. Galton walked the short distance to the sawmill where he worked and exchanged courtesies with the watchman he was to relieve.

EIGHT

On Sunday Galton went to inform Winston of his decision to marry. Jessie killed a chicken and Winston wanted to invite a neighbour whose acquaintanceship he had made only a few days before. But Galton objected and the celebration was confined to his friend's family circle. Winston embraced Jessie and recalled the day they were married. Their daughter Thelma, a frail girl of twelve who wore glasses with round lenses, looked on, not knowing what to make of her parents' enthusiasm for their friend's marriage. He was a grown man, who ought to have been married long ago.

"How many children you going to have? Eight, nine, ten?" Winston asked in jest.

"Two'll be enough," Galton replied.

"That's the trend," said his friend, shaking his head regretfully. "This country can hold thirty million people and still have lots of space. Two!"

A similar remark from Selwyn would have brought forth a sharp reaction from Galton, who merely smiled and said, "I'm not bringing children into the world for the country's sake. When I'm struggling to feed them the country won't notice. Besides, what sort of example you're setting, with one?"

"Thelma," said Jessie, addressing her daughter, "go and dry those things on the table for me."

Thelma got up slowly, reluctant to miss the rest of the conversation. When she believed her to be out of earshot Jessie observed, "Deciding is one thing, having them's another."

Thelma, who had pressed her ear against the partition that divided the kitchen from the dining area, heard the remark and the ensuing conversation on the advantages or otherwise of having a large family.

"People can have four, five children in this country," said Winston, "without going crazy. All children need is space."

"And companionship," added Jessie meaningfully.

In the short silence that followed Thelma tiptoed to the sink, fearing that her mother might come into the kitchen.

Winston began talking about engaged couples and newlyweds and Jessie listened intently. She knew that he made up half of his stories, but was nevertheless continually seduced by them.

The three talked until Jessie's mother, a woman in her sixties, came down to help cook the food. Jessie joined her in the kitchen and the two men went upstairs to inspect the rooms Galton and his new wife would use.

"When's she coming?" asked Winston, referring to Gemma.

"She'll write to tell me exactly what date," replied Galton.

"Bring her here as soon as she comes. Ma'll let you in. . . . Let's see," he reflected aloud. "I'll get a couple of keys made tomorrow and you can give her one. Well, that's settled."

The house had four bedrooms and had been put up a year ago some distance from the Public Road. Along with it had been built more than thirty others in concrete with flat roofs. Unlike the traditional mansions they had no outside staircases. Galton missed the Demerara windows, too, with their ornately carved sides and broad ledges. But, in their own way, they were attractive. He resolved to have one built for Gemma some time in the future. Contrary to his original intention, he had actually written her before he came to see Winston and her reply had come that morning. Her father had written as well, a long, emotional letter in which he declared his faith in Galton and the conviction that he would make his daughter happy. He was prepared to give any help Galton might need, financial or otherwise. Unfortunately, he would not be able to attend the wedding, since there was no one to look after the shop in his absence. The place was an institution, he claimed, and closing it, even for one day, was unthinkable.

So he, Galton Flood, was to get married, as his brother had and Winston; like his father and his grandfather. He was to be responsible for maintaining a household, and for its security. If an intruder got into the house *he* would have to face him. The manifold fears that beset so many young men on the threshold of marriage tortured him as he followed his friend through the rooms where he and his bride were to live. He would have liked to ask Winston a hundred and one questions—about intimacy with a woman especially; what was expected of him, whether it was proper to speak about the act with her, and many others.

"You see?" Winston said, pointing to the roof where it met the wall. "Water comes in there. These damned contractors! Most of them're illiterate. I kept back seven hundred dollars from what I owed him. It's not only this house, y'know. Half of the others're leaking too. Some of them even have fungus on the floor. Nobody! Nobody can match us for building in wood. I'm telling you. But what the hell do we know about concrete?"

They sat down on two straight-backed chairs on the veranda that ran the length of the house on the second storey and talked until Thelma came up to tell her father that lunch was ready.

Galton sat next to Jessie's mother, opposite Thelma and Jessie. Winston bent down over the old woman, who was almost deaf and shouted in her ear, "He's getting married!"

She turned to look at Galton with a broad smile.

"You must treat her good," she said.

"They're not married yet!" Jessie shouted over.

"What?" asked the old lady.

Winston shouted into her ear once more. "They're not married yet!"

"I know!" she exclaimed irritably. "I'm not deaf!"

Then he showed her three fingers as a sign that the couple would be married in three months' time and put his hand on her shoulder in an indulgent gesture.

"Come on. Daddy, I'm hungry!" Thelma complained. She was referring to the carving of the chicken. Winston set about his task expertly, so that in a few minutes everyone had a portion of the pale meat on his plate.

Meanwhile Jessie had shared out the steaming rice from the large bowl in the middle of the table. Besides, there were fried plantains, eddoes, tanias, sweet potatoes, baked snapper, dhalpourri and pigeon peas. The old lady bowed her head and said grace, but before she was quite finished Thelma had plunged her fork into the sweet potato in her plate.

"With all the food you eat you're still so fine," Jessie remarked. "If you ate less you might put on some weight."

Thelma adjusted her glasses and stared at her mother without answering.

It was the servant's day off and from time to time Jessie got up to take some plate or dish away, or to bring in the guava stew and the coconut water.

Galton could not help feeling envious of this household of three generations, where appetites were large and food was plentiful and the manifest harmony was an affront to the tensions and bitterness of other homes.

Winston fetched ice from the refrigerator and put two lumps into each glass of coconut water. He rounded off his meal with a long shot of rum, in which the ice cubes barely floated.

"My dear," said Winston to his wife, "rarely have I dined so well. I remember that afternoon two years ago when we gorged ourselves on curry beef. Now, that was a meal! But this was a meal to end all meals!"

He bent down and kissed her on her forehead.

"Ah, you always say that," declared Jessie, pretending to be indifferent.

"Is what he saying?" asked her mother.

"Our cooking was good!" shouted Jessie.

"He always say that," she remarked, and a smile of satisfaction replaced her normally severe look.

When Winston asked Thelma to fetch his box of cigars Jessie got up and began clearing the table. The two men went upstairs to talk on the veranda. Below them the garden beds were covered with low, flowering shrubs, which had only been put in since the house was completed. To the left, a few hundred yards away, the two minarets of a mosque rose above the trees.

"You lucky, y'know," said Galton to his friend. "Jessie and all this. Some men would give anything to be in your shoes."

"I suppose you're right," Winston answered. "We got married one Saturday afternoon in Golden Grove. Had to leave Thelma in town. She didn't know we weren't married and with her funny ways you never can tell what she would've got up to. Jessie was all for telling her the truth, but I preferred not to take the risk. You're worried, aren't you?"

"No. Why should I?" asked Galton.

"It'll soon rain, and Jessie's mother will get irritable and complain that Peter's Hall isn't like Golden Grove. One thing—I know you'd rather not discuss it, but whatever you do you must invite Nekka to the wedding. If you don't it will be a slap in Selwyn's face. You don't understand women: Nekka would be glad if you left her out, just to have the satisfaction of knowing you—"

Galton interrupted him sharply. "It's all very well for you to give advice. You've got a wife that idolises you, a house of your own. Forget! I've only got my pride, damn it!"

Winston got up and closed the door that led into the bedroom, so that the others would not hear what Galton was saying.

"Just for your pride you'd hurt Selwyn?"

Galton did not answer. A light breeze had sprung up and there were more grey clouds overhead. Galton reflected that he was prepared to invite a dozen Nekkas if he was assured that he had taken the right step in sending for Gemma.

Winston wanted to put his arm round Galton and reassure him, but he knew him well enough to leave him alone.

When the rain came down suddenly Winston involuntarily looked up at the spot where the leak was. He threw the cigar stump in the direction of the road and saw it fall on the grass verge, just beyond the stone wall. Little suspended globules of water were running along the sloping electric wires that connected the house to the lamp post until, fed by the rain, they fell like incandescent pearls to the concrete below. It was like David Street, thought Galton, when the afternoon was heavy with the sound of falling rain, and he watched the moisture-laden oleander drooping across the paling.

Gemma's letter accepting his proposal had been different from the earlier ones. The tone was more submissive and she had not once used the word "tormentor." Now he recognised that it was not Nekka, nor the house, nor the prospect of settling in Winston's home that was bothering him. It was Gemma's compliant letter. While before writing to her he had been looking forward to their union, he was now filled with apprehension.

"Nobody should be allowed to build a house with a flat roof," said Winston. "The minimum gradient should be laid down by law; say, one in twenty-five."

He got up and passed his hand over the spot where he expected the water to come in, but it was still dry.

The two friends continued to exchange bits of conversation, while the rain fell fitfully. Galton left in the late afternoon, accompanied by the whistling of frogs from the recently cleared land and the vision of Winston's three fingers signifying the number of months that remained to him as a single man.

NINE

The hooting of the first car that turned off the public road in Peter's Hall attracted the attention of passers-by. The strips of white ribbon converging to meet at the tip of its hood and the yellow cloth at the base of the window indicated that the occupants were coming from a wedding. In quick succession several other cars, more or less lavishly decorated, came by and the women on the road looked eagerly at each of them to see if they could spot the bride; but the cars drove past so quickly that only those standing at the turning, where the vehicles were obliged to slow down, were able to see Gemma, austere in satin and white lace, hunched in the rear of the second car.

Puffing on his thick cigar, Winston was welcoming the guests at the gate. Galton experienced his first pang of jealousy when he saw his friend kiss his new wife on both cheeks.

There had been no rain for two days and many of the guests stayed outside with Winston to chat. He assured them that he liked his new house and denied that he was a rich man, underlining his assertion with a mighty puff on his cigar. He then declared aloud his intention to take Jessie away on another honeymoon.

When Selwyn arrived with Nekka Winston quietly drew her aside and urged her to be pleasant with Galton. Pretending she did not know what he was talking about she asked to go and see the presents, then, taking her husband's arm, went into the house with the waddling gait of a woman in the advanced state of pregnancy. In fact her condition was barely evident.

Selwyn was offended that Galton had chosen Winston to be his best man, but was determined not to raise the matter. He caught sight of his brother standing beside Gemma, who was sitting in an armchair by the door. The brothers introduced their wives to each other. Nekka, who appeared to be embarrassed, giggled at everything Selwyn said.

"You see the presents yet?" she asked Gemma.

"Of course she's seen them! They're hers!" Selwyn reminded her.

"I don't know what get into me. I feel as if I been drinking," she went on.

Gemma stared at Nekka, who looked round her as if in search of someone.

"You'd better come upstairs," Selwyn suggested.

Nekka jumped at the suggestion and accompanied him up the spiral staircase to the bedroom where the gifts were laid out on a large bed. A number of women were standing about the room, talking or examining the presents. There were cutlery and crockery, sheets encased in plastic covers, two electric irons, pillow cases, an electric toaster and a variety of other household goods. The collection was no different from that displayed on similar occasions, but the curiosity aroused was as intense and the remarks as predictable.

Nekka took Selwyn aside and whispered, "I don't like she."

"Who?" he asked.

"Galton wife."

"Why?"

"She . . . I don't know," answered Nekka, at some pains to find a reason for not liking Gemma. "She mek me skin go all . . . ," and Nekka shuddered to demonstrate what she meant.

"She don't like me," she then added.

"What you expect if you ask her stupid questions," retorted Selwyn.

"I din' know what to say. She got eyes like a cat in the dark," said Nekka.

She nudged him when they were approached by Jessie, who said, "Come downstairs and have a drink, ne? Winston was looking for you."

Jessie took Nekka by the hand and led her out of the room, followed by Selwyn.

"Who's looking after the baby?" Jessie asked.

"The neighbour."

"She should've come too," said Jessie.

"She couldn't lef' the others. Tobesides, her husband wouldn't let her," answered Nekka.

At the head of the staircase she held Selwyn's arm for support.

"They're a nice couple, eh?" observed Jessie, referring to Gemma and Galton.

"She's damn good-looking," Selwyn remarked.

"I'm coming just now. I just want to get the others downstairs," Jessie said.

Downstairs the guests from the nine cars were talking in groups. Galton had expressly forbidden Winston to hire musicians or to prepare a big meal because, he declared, he could not afford it. But Winston protested when Galton would have dispensed with the cake-cutting ceremony. The latter gave in, provided that neither Winston nor anyone else made a speech.

When Winston announced that the cake was to be cut there was a rustling of dresses and a scraping of chairs. If few of the guests knew Galton no one knew Gemma, so that the affair was turning out to be more a party given by Winston, whose resonant laughter echoed round the house.

"Is who making the speech?" asked a man wearing a white shirt-jack.

"Come on, Winston! Speech!" a woman exclaimed.

Winston threw up his arms in an appeal for silence.

"No speech," he said, when there was silence. "No speech."

There was a concerted "Oh!" of disappointment from the guests.

"*I'm* going to make a speech," said the man in the shirt-jack, and sprang forward. But Winston restrained him.

"No, the bridegroom doesn't want a speech," Winston said apologetically. Whereupon, everyone turned to look at Galton, whose embarrassment was painfully obvious. He got the impression that he was surrounded by the whole population of Georgetown, who were staring at him and his wife; and the silence . . . the awful silence of thirty-odd people who, a moment ago were laughing and calling out for a speech. In that interminable moment beads of sweat appeared on Galton's forehead. Gemma, on the other hand, was looking at the gathering defiantly. Her breathing was even and her right hand rested lightly on her husband's arm.

"What we waiting for?" asked Selwyn.

The couple stepped forward and Gemma took up the knife which lay on the table next to the three-tiered cake. She turned towards Galton, smiled and then kissed him long and passionately *before* cutting the cake. One woman, unable to contain her surprise, exclaimed, "Eh, eh!"

Nekka pressed her knee against Selwyn's leg without looking at him. When Gemma, assisted by Galton, sliced through the cake, there was an "Ah!" from the women. Jessie then cut the cake into large portions and passed them to Thelma who, in turn, distributed them to those around her.

After the guests had dispersed throughout the drawing-room and the dining area the talk was almost exclusively about Gemma's behaviour.

"Imagine cutting the cake after kissing! Well, I never!"

"I hear she come from Wismar," said another.

"Naw, naw! Is from Linden," observed yet another.

"Is the same, Wismar and McKenzie; they both call Linden now. Is only eight cents to cross the river."

"You hear her talk yet? As if she so superior, with words nobody else does use. And her father does only run a cake shop! Is who she fooling?"

The guests were disappointed that there was to be no dancing. One of them tried to get a party game started, but without success. Winston, fearing that they would go home, began telling ribald stories to a group of men who were standing in the middle of the drawing-room. Soon they were joined by others, both men and women, and even Galton left Gemma, who was talking to Jessie, to go and listen to his friend. When he could take no more he went outside and leaned on the new wrought-iron gate. He surveyed the line of cars in the unnamed street and reflected that, like all of his kind, he would be expected to have a car by the time he was thirty, just as he was expected to get married. No doubt he would see that his children had private lessons, as Thelma was having, in order to ensure a free place at secondary school. To do all this he would be obliged to limit his family to two children. Gemma would realise all this quickly and offer him a haven at Wismar. Now, since he was prepared to make a home in the bush with her there ought to be no objection to living at Wismar where he need have no car, could bring up his children as he wished and would, by and large, be free of all the pressures and constraints that were exerted upon him here. But, as before, Galton dismissed the idea.

The air was damp, and the branches of the few palms that had not been cut down to make room for the new houses, hung limp beneath a threatening sky. Occasionally there was a burst of laughter from inside, like sounds from another world. Turning to look at the house he saw figures of guests behind the louvred glass windows. What difference would Gemma make to his life? He loved her. As to that there was no longer any doubt. He loved her too much, in fact, and was more afraid than ever of the consequences of this formal coupling that began in a church he never attended, in the presence of a gathering with whom he had little in common. He loved her for her warm hands, for the incongruity of her ways, for her fearlessness, and desired to have her pregnant every year, so that she would be entirely dependent on him.

When he went back inside he heard Selwyn, who had joined Winston's group, say, "It won't be long before we start celebrating divorces, having real celebrations with food and rum." Here he raised his plate of chow-mien to emphasise his point.

"The parting couple'd invite their friends and we'd laugh and talk like now and I. . . ."

"Only a man could say that," observed a woman with some bitterness.

"If there wasn't any marriage there wouldn't need to be divorce," put in Winston. "Probably they'll abolish marriage. After all it's abolishing itself bit by bit."

"And what about the women who're saddled with children?" asked the woman.

"Wha. . . ."

"If. . . ."

Winston and Selwyn began to speak at the same time.

"What about them?" Winston asked. "The state would recognise their special position and support them until the children grew up."

"Ah! I was waiting for that," said the woman, her lips pursed and speaking with passion. "While the man gets off scot-free."

Galton went to look for Gemma, who was no longer standing where he had left her. One or two others drew away as well, uneasy at the turn the conversation was taking. Selwyn tried to soothe the woman, but his words had the opposite effect.

"It was just a suggestion," he said. "What d'you suggest then?"

"Why should I suggest anything?" the woman asked.

"I know you women . . ." began Selwyn.

"Me? What do you know about me?" she shrieked.

Jessie came hurrying up.

"Stella! Come away, come away," she urged, taking the woman's arm. But the latter wrenched herself free.

"What do you know about me?" she repeated, thrusting her right arm forward in hostile fashion.

Nekka, still clutching her plate of food, was looking on. Selwyn's attention was drawn to the black gloves the woman was wearing. The sight of this unusual attire, more than anything else, moved him to say, "I'm sorry."

In answer, the woman rushed forward and seized the collar of his shirt.

"You don't know anything about me!" she screamed at the top of her voice.

By the time Jessie, Winston and another man had pulled her away from Selwyn, his plate had been knocked to the floor and the food in it scattered around him. Only the lowest button on his shirt front was still intact and his dark, hairless chest was half-exposed.

The woman was led away towards the back of the house by Jessie and Winston, who came back a little later with a shirt in his hand. He gave it to Selwyn. The latter, still looking slightly bewildered, took off his own and put the new one on.

They were to learn later from Jessie that the woman had twice been married to the same man. After the divorce from him she threatened to harm herself if he did not come back to her. As a result of the injury to her hands—no one seemed to know how she came by it—he remarried her, but divorced her yet again a few years later.

All the gaiety had gone out of the reception. Those who were still eating were doing so more deliberately, as if they had lost their appetite; and those engaged in conversation were murmuring.

When Jessie's mother was told what had happened she said, "Is a bad sign when people quarrel at a wedding. Is a bad sign. And they're such a nice couple. Decent. All this talking don't do nobody no good. Look at them!" she exclaimed, nodding in the direction of the guests. "You'd think the world would come to a end if they stop talking."

Some time later the woman who had attacked Selwyn was taken home by Winston. The guests began to leave as early as eight o'clock and by ten everyone had gone. Winston, Galton, Jessie, Gemma and Jessie's mother sat around the dining-table discussing the night's events. Gemma had changed into a plain dress, which made her look less forbidding. Jessie looked drawn and declared that she was tired and would go to bed early. Nevertheless, they talked until nearly midnight, when Jessie's mother was the first to retire.

Winston said, "She wasn't invited, you know." The others knew he was referring to the woman he had taken home.

"What?" Galton asked.

"I didn't invite her," declared Winston, turning to Jessie.

"Neither did I," said Jessie.

"Whose car did she come in?" asked Galton.

Winston questioned Jessie with a look, but she only shrugged her shoulders.

"Can't understand it," said Winston, a perturbed note in his voice.

"I can," observed Gemma.

The other three looked at her.

"What d'you mean?" asked Jessie.

"I can understand why she came," continued Gemma, "and after all it wasn't hard to get in."

"There weren't more than thirty people," said Jessie.

"Oh, it's not important," Galton declared. "I was glad it happened."

"You would!" exclaimed Winston. "If you'd allowed me to have music it wouldn't have come to it."

"Something was bound to get broken if we'd been dancing," put in Jessie, suppressing a yawn.

"You're all looking bleary-eyed," observed Winston, "and this is just the time I'm ready to talk and smoke all night."

Jessie got up, stretched and said goodnight to Galton and Gemma, who got up as well.

"Sleep well and tell me tomorrow if you liked the rooms," said Winston, who followed his wife upstairs.

"We must get out of this house," whispered Gemma when Jessie and Winston were upstairs.

"I know," replied Galton, staring past her into the darkness outside.

She approached him, laid her head against his chest and let him support her body; and they stood by the window where the night air came in through the half-closed louvres. The young shrubs were shadowless in the high beds, somehow incongruous in Peter's Hall where, until a year ago, only vegetables were cultivated in small, subsistence plots.

Overhead, the sound of an aeroplane came and went, fading away to the north and the ocean. Gemma and Galton went up to bed in this the first night of their marriage.

TEN

Gemma was sitting on the bed, her knees tucked under her chin. She watched for the slightest movement made by Galton, who was standing with his back to her. It was about two in the morning and the night silence was broken only by the occasional sound of a car from the public road.

The couple had not spoken to each other for several minutes.

"It's not the first time, is it?" asked Galton.

After a moment's hesitation she replied. "No. Does it mean so much to you? I'm. . . ."

He interrupted her. "It means a lot to me, especially with you."

"Oh."

Again, for several minutes there was nothing said. The stillness was disturbed by the noise of rushing water from the water closet at the head of the staircase.

"There're no dogs in Peter's Hall. I wonder why," Galton said absently.

"Neither in Wismar," she rejoined. "At least not so many as in town."

He went and sat at the foot of the bed.

"Who was it?" he asked.

She did not answer and he turned towards her.

"Someone who used to come and see Pa. He was in his forties. . . ."

"How d'you mean 'was'?" enquired Galton.

"He's in the bush now. He goes from time to time," she answered. "He's ugly, grey and's got yellow teeth. He took to coming to the house when Pa was away in the shop. I used to leave him alone in the drawing-room, reading. He read nothing but Rosicrucian literature and magazines on psychology. I hated him for his habits: he never cleaned his nails and when I mentioned this once he told me to bring the scissors and cut them for him. I flew into a rage and asked him if he thought I was his servant. . . ."

She fell silent when she realised she was being carried away.

"Go on," Galton ordered. "Go on!" He had felt a wave of excitement at Gemma's account and his disappointment at the brusque interruption was almost physical.

"He ignored what I said and told me again to bring the scissors. I wasn't myself, Galton. I did what he told me and cut his long, ugly nails with the dirt underneath. He didn't even touch me then. It was later; one day when it was so hot I opened all the windows and fell asleep on the bed. I dreamt that someone was taking off my skin, layer by layer, and I didn't feel any pain. When I woke up he was sitting on the bed. . . ." She interrupted what she was saying to look up at Galton and saw that he was listening intently.

"He was sitting on the bed," she continued, "stroking my head. And . . . I was somehow too sleepy to resist . . . the

heat and the droning of the black marabuntas . . . and the
sun on the wall . . . the sun on the wall . . . I was so lonely!
All my friends had gone away to Georgetown or abroad,
and I had lost all shame. When I told you in my letter
not to write me it was out of shame. After that afternoon
I started to treat him like an animal. I made him run
errands for me and clean the house and the yard and the
brass. I thought—at the time I thought there was something extraordinary about him, because of the things he
read. But he was weak and tame. He did anything I said
just to have me again. . . . You should've come and taken
me away."

"You make me sick," Galton said. "The Walk-Man was
right about your father."

"What about him?"

"He didn't have to say anything. Your father was always
asking how I felt about you."

Gemma heaved a deep sigh.

"Is it important?" she asked. "What is important is the
way we treat each other."

"It is important to me. I . . . to me it's the whole basis
of our relationship."

In the ensuing silence Gemma no longer followed her
husband with her eyes. She had anticipated this situation
and had considered the desirability of writing Galton about
her experience with the ugly man.

Galton had memorised every word of a letter she had
written him, in which she reminded him that separation
was not the end of the world.

Had she foreseen this? he wondered. Then she must
have deliberately deceived him into marrying her!

He then recalled that it was only a few weeks ago that he had proposed marriage to her, having left her in a limbo of uncertainty all these years. The more deeply he thought of the matter the more he became lost in a web of arguments for and against her behaviour.

Weeks passed and the wound to Galton's pride healed gradually. Gemma sensed that he disliked Winston's little attentions, like the trips up the stairs with her shopping bag or his offers to run her to town in his car. She therefore discouraged them and on one occasion told him that Galton did not approve of this brotherly interest in her. She herself could see no more than that in Winston's conduct.

Both Winston and Jessie were of the opinion that Galton was too possessive. Winston had always behaved like that towards women and was certain that they and their men understood it. The incident, some years ago, when a man abused him for kissing his wife on the cheek was forgotten. That was his, Winston's, manner and any woman or man who took exception to it must be unsocial.

The slight rift was to grow larger with time. There were misunderstandings about Thelma, who sometimes stood outside the couple's door listening for any interesting bits of conversation. Jessie would have dealt with her severely if she had known, but to Gemma and Galton it provided more evidence for their belief that the girl was spoiled. She was allowed to remain in the drawing-room when grown-ups were chatting about people's personal affairs and to contribute to a conversation unsuitable for someone her age.

Difficulties also arose about sharing the kitchen and dividing the sweeping and cleaning between Jessie and Gemma. Were it not for the fact that the two women liked each other, matters would have come to a head in the weeks immediately following their marriage.

Meanwhile Galton had found a job in a radio repair workshop. The course he was following stood him in good stead, so that within a relatively short time he came to be regarded as a competent workman. When it was clear that Gemma would have to work to supplement his income she secured a job selling in one of the big stores.

Galton could not complain of the fare his wife set before him, for their joint incomes allowed them to eat well. The compensation Selwyn paid for use of the whole house was almost the same as the rent Galton paid Winston, and what was left over after these two basic needs had been met was enough to satisfy their way of life. But the contrast between Winston's table and his was so apparent that he was ashamed of it. He found himself dreading Winston's outbursts of laughter, especially when he and Gemma were alone in their rooms upstairs.

One night, recalling her words, *We must get out of this house*, he said to her: "We can't stay here long."

"Why?" Gemma asked, looking up from her ironing.

"I can't take it any more."

"I don't see why not. Like this we could save some money and in a few years put down on a small place."

At these words Galton was seized with a sort of panic.

"Only a few months ago you said . . ." he managed to mutter.

"What did I say?" she asked, carefully folding a shirt and placing it on a pile of ironed garments. All the difficulties marriage had presented to him while still a bachelor had proved to be more illusory than real. The one he had not foreseen had turned out to be a spectre haunting his two rooms, appearing with a single word, conjured up by laughter from downstairs, prowling in the corridor that separated the bedrooms of the two families.

"What did I say?" she repeated.

"Nothing," he answered.

Gemma saw in Galton a saviour, who had transported her from Linden to the teeming world of Georgetown. She idolised him for the superiority with which she herself had invested him and saw him as the catalyst by means of which she could transform herself. His poverty, far from being an obstacle to advancement, provided the challenge that would fire her ambition. Success for herself interested her little, unless achieved through him and with him. She was therefore disappointed at his display of jealousy. Moreover, it was unworthy of Galton to be jealous of a man like Winston.

She was surprised that Galton spent so much time doing nothing, not even reading a book or listening to the radio. Once he had worked through his radio correspondence lesson he was content to throw his leg over the easy-chair and watch her perform the household duties. Before she left Linden she was of the opinion that Georgetonians spent their time reading and generally bettering themselves.

"Georgetown people don't let grass grow under their feet," was one of her father's favourite remarks.

However, it was too early in their marriage to think of changing Galton. She was convinced that he needed her and, in spite of his moodiness, in spite of his demands for privacy, was very close to her. He had insisted that she wear her underclothes in bed, even during their acts of intimacy, but these were small matters in the greater design of their living together.

Gemma watched him and was afraid of losing him. Why could he not help her iron and fold the linen? The act of working together would cement their relationship, which was growing like some fragile plant, in danger of being throttled by others more vigorous.

Yes, she thought, *we must go away from here; anywhere, so long as we're alone.*

"We must go away from here," she said aloud.

"Yes," Galton retorted, as if he did not care.

A few minutes later they heard Winston's voice. He had come home from a Lodge meeting, accompanied by some friends. When Gemma heard him she looked up at Galton, who caught her eye and experienced the same access of hostility towards her that he had felt for Nekka after overhearing that she wanted him out of the house. Gemma was on the point of saying something, but knew that any remark would only make matters worse. She continued ironing until the unironed heap had disappeared. When, at last, she went to bed, he remained in his chair long after Winston's friends had gone home and the house was filled with silence.

ELEVEN

The following evening Galton came home reeking of liquor.

"What got in your head to start drinking?" Gemma asked him.

"Pack your things! We're leaving this house now!" he exclaimed.

"Why?" Gemma asked.

"We're going now!"

"Where?"

"I don't know," he answered.

"We can't go without knowing where we're going," she protested.

"That's what I expected. You mean you don't want to leave this house, you slut!"

Gemma looked at him in disbelief.

"Pack your things," he said in an even voice.

She sank into one of the straight-backed chairs at the dining-table, while Galton opened the door and saw Thelma turn away. He brushed past her as if he had expected her to be there and when he came back from the bathroom did not even notice that she was gone.

"Be sensible, Galton," Gemma said to him on his return.

He opened the bottom drawer of the chest-of-drawers and started to pull out his shirts. Realising that he was serious she pushed him aside gently and continued to empty the drawers. If they were to move, so be it.

The packing took considerably longer than she had anticipated and, in the end, they realised that at least two trips would be needed to move the things to their new home. But Galton persisted in his intention to drag her out first and come back for all their household goods later. The couple left empty-handed. At the foot of the staircase they were met by Jessie, who was near to tears.

"Thelma say you been quarrelling about us," Jessie ventured.

Gemma looked back at Thelma, who was standing at the kitchen door, peering through her glasses.

"Not about you," said Gemma.

"You're leaving?" she asked.

"Yes," Galton replied. "Tell Winston I'll be coming back for the things, probably tomorrow."

"But why? Did we do you anything? Thelma! Come here! Don't be afraid to tell me if she did anything. Her father'll attend to her."

"We're sorry to go," said Gemma, "But . . . it's. . . . Nobody did anything."

"Why not wait till Winston comes home?" suggested Jessie. "He could give you a lift in the car."

"No, we'll be all right," Galton said firmly.

Thelma ran upstairs to watch them go through the gate. As they turned the corner she came out on the balcony, boldly showing herself and waving to the couple, who could only see her if they turned round. Then, taking out her skipping rope from a cupboard in her parents' room—where it had been hidden as a punishment—she went downstairs and out of the house. She began skipping in the middle of the unlit street, accompanying each hop with, "Ayree, doree, tilya, chowree, zampa, zed, zoota," in succession, beginning again until she had exhausted the seven words.

The commotion and the couple's departure had occurred without Jessie's mother's knowledge. When Jessie disclosed what had happened, her mother said, "There was quarrelling at the reception. I did tell you."

Jessie feared, above all, that the close links between her household and Galton might be impaired, indeed severed by his going away.

She went upstairs and pushed open the door of the couple's room. Two suitcases lay on the floor, their lids wide open. On the table was an assortment of crockery, boxes and books and a clock, which could not find a place in the luggage on the floor. Jessie knew that the arrangement could not last, but the evidence that it had come to an end left her with a feeling of uneasiness. Whose fault was it? Hers? Winston's? Thelma's? Or even her mother's?

"Thelma!" she called out, and heard her daughter opening the gate.

"What you did to Galton and Gemma?" Jessie asked, when her daughter was standing before her.

"Nothing!" exclaimed Thelma, opening her eyes wide.

"And where you got this skipping rope from?" said Jessie, snatching the rope from her daughters hand. "My God! I don't know why you don't mind your own business. They probably caught you listening outside their door. You know what happens to children who tell lies? They go to sleep and don't wake up again."

Jessie grabbed her daughter by the shoulders and shook her.

"What did you do?" asked Jessie again. Then, in exasperation, she let go.

That night, when there was the sound of a car pulling up, Jessie hurried to the front door, expecting to see Winston. It was Galton, who had come back in a taxi for his things. She opened the door and could no longer hold the words back.

"What did we do you?"

Galton was taken aback more by her manner than the question she asked.

"Nothing, I told you."

"How d'you think Winston'll take it?"

"I don't care how the devil Winston takes it. Who the hell is Winston?" replied Galton.

"I see."

"I've got a hired car waiting," said Galton, leaving her in the gallery. He made several trips upstairs to fetch the books and other odds and ends. Finally, he came down with a stack of books in his hand.

"I gone," he said to Jessie and stopped in the doorway.

"When you're coming to see us?" she asked.

"Soon, probably," he replied in as kindly a tone as possible. He then walked off to the waiting car.

Thelma was peeping at him from behind the blinds upstairs. The car drove away and before it could turn the corner, crossed Winston's car, which drew up in front of the gate.

TWELVE

It was weeks before Galton found a room. When Gemma followed him through the passage that led from Lombard Street pavement she was revolted by the squalor and asked, "It's here we're going to live?"

"Yes," Galton replied. She followed him up the creaking staircase to the second floor of the tenement.

"In here," he said, putting down the suitcase he was carrying. The smell made Gemma recoil, but Galton pretended that he noticed nothing. Without bothering to look back he went over to the single window and opened it.

It was a Sunday evening and the sound of hymn singing came from a radio somewhere above them.

"That's the coal-pot," said Galton, as he bent down to pick up an ancient coal-pot from a corner. "The landlord's putting in gas in a few months."

"How long'll we be living here?" enquired Gemma calmly.

"Until we find somewhere decent."

He took an electric bulb from his pocket, screwed it into the socket, then turned the light on. The bulb lit up the corners in which was a variety of litter the previous tenant had left behind.

"The man who lived here died a few days ago. He slept on the newspapers," Galton said.

A child began to scream and immediately the voice of a woman shrieked out, "Shut yo' rass! You lil bastard!"

The crying was reduced to a whimper. Galton avoided Gemma's eyes, angry that she said nothing conciliatory.

"People born and die in places like this!" Galton said indignantly. "If you don't like it take a bus tomorrow and go back to Linden."

"If you want to stay here I'll stay here too," said Gemma.

"In this filth?" asked Galton.

"D'you want to go back to the boarding-house?"

"We'd have to leave in a few weeks in any case," he replied, "With what we've got left."

"Then we'll stay, Galton."

Galton found out where the bathroom and toilet were and made friends with a man living on the first floor, who suggested that he come to him if ever he needed anything.

"If I was you I'd fumigate the room," he advised. "The man living there use to work in the sewers. That's why he get sick; din' eat enough. You could smell he as soon as he open his door and the air come out."

. The next morning Galton bought some formalin and disinfectant to fumigate the room. He had not told Gemma what their neighbour had said, fearing that she might want to go back to the boarding-house.

That afternoon, while he was lifting the new mattress through the passage a man called out, "Galton!" It was the watchman who had worked with him at the sawmill in Water Street. Galton invited him up and was glad that he came.

On hearing that he was married the watchman asked, "And you bring you wife to live here?" He stared at Galton incredulously.

Galton told him about his new job and his ambition to own his own radio shop.

"Careful wit' the chap downstairs," warned the watchman. "He's a police informer. Does stay home all day. In a couple of days he going come poking he nose in you room. If you don't give him coffee he going ask for it. Wait and see! He going pick up everything in the room and look under it and behind it. Everybody in the tenement frighten of him. Don' encourage him, that's the main thing."

Galton remembered his neighbour's suggestion that he should come to him if he needed anything. The man had seemed genuinely pleasant.

"You won't stay hey long, though," observed the watchman.

"Why?" asked Galton.

"A couple visits from the police and you won't be able to tek it any more."

"Why should the police come here?"

"Stolen goods, man. They always searching hey. You come to the right place for live."

Galton shrugged his shoulders with feigned indifference.

"And tobesides," added the watchman, "nobody going come and visit you here."

Galton began to roll a cigarette. At the time he was working at the sawmill he and the watchman used to exchange the barest courtesies. In fact the latter had never strung a whole sentence together for him. The appearance of Galton in the twilight world of thieves and receivers was proof enough that they were on the same footing. He spoke as freely as if he were engaging a neighbour or a relation in conversation. For Galton's part, the months he worked at the sawmill were, in retrospect, a time of calm, when he could lie down on his bench and fall asleep under the stars, when, in the long nights, the chugging of boats on the river broke the monotony of the passing hours.

A cockroach scurried across the room; the watchman took off his shoe and slew it with a blow.

The two men sat in silence.

"You know anything about Wismar?" Galton asked the watchman.

"Been there once, that's all. Why?"

"Just for so. I know someone from Wismar," said Galton.

"Tek the day off, eh?"

"They gave me it for the moving," Galton replied. "I never found out where you're living."

"The Ruimveldt Housing Scheme," said the watchman. "The town getting so big! Twenty years ago you could walk from one end to the other in three-quarter hour."

The two men talked until Gemma came home from work, when the watchman got up and addressed her with "Miss," introducing himself as "a old friend of Mr Galton."

Gemma prepared fried fish, bread and coffee and the guest insisted on going downstairs to fetch water, with which they washed their hands.

After the watchman left Gemma took the cups and plates down to the yard and washed them. She and Galton lay down on the mattress and talked until she fell asleep, exhausted from the long hours on her feet in the place she worked.

Late that night the couple were awakened by stamping in the room above them.

"Is my money!" a woman shouted.

"Is mine, you whore!" came a man's voice.

"Is who you calling a whore? You think I is you mother?"

There was the sound of breaking glass. The quarrel raged until more voices were heard, but the truce did not last for long and when the dispute broke out afresh there was a violent slamming of a door, followed by hurried foot-steps on the stairs.

"You frightened?" Galton asked Gemma.

"No," she answered quickly.

For her Georgetown meant Peter's Hall, Lombard Street and Water Street, where she worked. Everything that happened around her must be normal; if others were not alarmed she need not be.

Early the next morning the coughing coming from a room across the corridor woke Galton and almost imme-diately an infant in the room above began to bawl. Galton got up, rolled a cigarette then opened the window which overlooked an alleyway. A man who was urinating against the paling looked up at him and looked down again. A few stars were still palely visible in a sky that promised another sweltering day. The man skipped over the gutter that ran down the middle of the alleyway and walked off in the direction of La Penitence. Galton wanted to draw a glass of water, but remembered that there was no sink in the room. Instead, he lit his cigarette, leaned against the window frame and watched his wife sleeping.

Since coming back to Georgetown his most satisfying hours had been spent in the company of the watchman, who, indeed, was little more than a stranger. A statement he had made kept coming back like some nagging dream.

"When you find out why you become a watchman you going find out why you bring you wife to live in this room."

"We couldn't find anything," Galton had answered. "Why you think I could find anything quicker than anybody else?"

He reflected that he had never heard of anyone who had taken a wife to live in the same house as a friend. What had, in truth, driven him to expose his young wife to the humiliation of sharing another man's furniture in another man's house? Gemma herself had told him, the first night of their marriage, "We must get out of this house." She was not the complaining kind; but he had allowed her words to go unheeded.

For the first time in months Galton thought of his mother. The tacit truce that had existed between her and his father went back almost as far as he could remember and was broken only occasionally by violent outbreaks of temper on his mother's part. In fact, his earliest memory was of his mother belabouring his father in a frenzy of anger. He recalled how he looked on, paralysed with fear, and how, afterwards, he wanted the world to come to an end. He was only three then. Other memories went back to the age of five or six, recollections of little consequence that cluttered his mind; like the day he passed the funeral parlour for the first time and saw the highly polished coffins arranged neatly in a room adjoining the public parlour; or the day he stole a ride on a passing dray-cart; or when he offered the girl who lived next door a star-picture in exchange for a kiss.

Gemma tossed on the mattress and Galton put out his cigarette. The sound of horses' hooves came from the street where the traffic was beginning to announce the dawn. If he lay down there would not be enough time to fall asleep; if he fetched water from downstairs and washed he might wake Gemma.

The coughing and crying had ceased, but in the room upstairs, where there had been fighting the night before someone was moving about. A few minutes later a man was coming down the stairs, apparently two or three at a time. Gemma turned on her side and a few moments later opened her eyes. They talked for a while, then she left the room to fetch water and take a bath. Galton knew that she would be long, for both the shower bath in the house and the one in the yard were likely to be occupied at that time of the morning.

The room was already stuffy from the heat of the new day and the little light that entered cruelly exposed its walls, grey from years of neglect.

THIRTEEN

Galton heard of a six-month radio course being run at the Young Men's Christian Association in Upper Camp Street. It had begun two weeks before, but as he was already in the trade his late application was accepted. He told Gemma that the lessons were the most instructive he had ever followed on the subject and every Tuesday night he was the first to take his place in the large back room of the building. The lesson lasted two hours, but, as the teacher was invariably late, Galton hardly ever got away before a quarter to ten.

Never since his marriage had he spoken so much to Gemma. The instructor possessed a sound theoretical and practical knowledge of transistors and, above all, managed to put over his subject in simple terms. She heard about emitters, bases and collectors, about negative and positive conduction and about the function of semi-conductors. He explained the difference between radios with tubes and transistors and why the latter could be built much smaller than the former.

In the months that followed his enthusiasm increased rather than diminished and he claimed that he had learned more in the last three months than in all the time that had preceded the course.

One night, just as he was about to leave for the YMCA, there was a knock on the door. Gemma opened.

"Eh, eh, Miss Flood, I just come to pay all you a social visit of sorts."

It was the neighbour from the room below, about whom the watchman had warned them.

Gemma looked round at Galton, who was standing behind her.

"I'm going out. Tell him to come another time," said Galton.

The man stepped inside, smiling affably.

"Is only me, Mr Flood; is only me."

Gemma drew back and the two men were left facing each other.

"You'll have to come back another time," Galton said firmly.

The neighbour scratched his temple, stepped further in and walked past both of them.

"I come to borrow some sugar, Mr Flood. I say to meself is he going lend you the sugar, not them that been living hey long."

All the while he was grinning. Gemma, in a sudden movement, went over to the table and undid the lid of a tin in which she kept the sugar; then, tearing off a piece of brown paper that was rolled up beside the tin of condensed milk, she poured about a handful of the brown crystals into it and handed the packet to the neighbour.

"That was quick. I was telling me sister when you come that this tenement going up, not down. I. . . ." But at that point Galton opened the door as widely as he could. The neighbour coughed, smiling at the same time.

"Well, I kian' complain. I come for sugar and I get sugar. The Lord don't forget that sort of thing. And we Guyanese is good Christians."

With that he left the room, bearing away the borrowed sugar.

"Such barefaced . . . !" exclaimed Galton, when he had closed the door. He stood, a puzzled expression on his face. His hand was still on the door knob.

"I can't understand it," he muttered.

"You'd better go; you'll be late," Gemma urged him, but he only left reluctantly. Although it was early the tenement was unusually still as if all the children and women were out. In the deserted alleyway a newspaper page ran fitfully along the gutter, propelled by a warm wind that had been blowing all afternoon and had brought a sultry, depressing air to the town.

"Oh, my God!" exclaimed Gemma softly.

At Wismar she saw everything from her window: the launches coming and going across the river, their bows lifted above the water, the rubbish cart with its covered top, and people, most of whom she knew. Beneath the sole window in this room was the alleyway, strewn with rubbish deposited in the night, with its gutter and its dilapidated palings and corrugated iron.

Why was she afraid of the neighbour? "Damn it!" she thought, "I don't have to be afraid of him."

Despite the incident, and the fact that the informer never bothered to give him back the sugar he had borrowed, Galton and he got to talking quite often. Sometimes

Galton would stop on the way up the stairs and chat with him through his window; and once Gemma came home to find them in earnest conversation. Her husband was sitting on the stairs while their neighbour, hands in his pockets, was listening intently to what Galton was saying. When she asked him later what they had to talk about Galton replied that he never liked stopping, but that in the end it was always worth it.

"What d'you talk about?" she insisted.

"I don't know. Anything. . . . I don't like him, but if you refused to talk to everybody you didn't like. . . ."

"But you don't stand for hours with people you don't like."

"People can't explain all their actions, can they?" Galton asked. "At least I can't. He's got a mind like a cess-pool, but he knows a lot about life."

"Oh!" Gemma said, raising her hand in exasperation.

"Why're you so obsessed with him? You don't miss an opportunity to run him down," Galton remarked.

"Run him down! You yourself said he's got a mind like a cess-pool."

"I don't know. You're right. But remember, I don't stop to talk to him: it's he who puts his head out of the window and starts. If everyone did that once a day the world might even be a better place."

"Might it?" Gemma asked.

Gemma smiled and Galton returned her smile. Latterly he seemed more contented than he had ever been since their move to the tenement. He hardly referred to his brother Selwyn or to Nekka, his wife, the mention of whose name was once sufficient to put him out of sorts for a whole day.

One night later that week Galton was again stopped on the stairs by the informer. "Eh, Mr Galton, come in for a drink, ne. Moma!" he called out; and before Galton had time to make an excuse his hand was taken by a lady in her fifties.

"Hello, sweetheart," she said to Galton. "Come in, ne. He tell me 'bout you; and is true what he say: you got sad eyes."

She kissed Galton full on his lips and pressed her body against his. For him, it was like embracing the old vaudeville artist who lived next door to the family house in Kitty.

"No, thanks, I don't drink," Galton apologised, when the informer tried to put a glass into his hand.

"Get him a soft drink. You come and talk to me in the corner, sweetheart. I like sitting in dark corners. Sit down there. What you name?"

"Galton."

"Galton? I never meet a Galton before," said the informer's mother.

Then, looking about her as if to make certain they were not being overheard she whispered, "He in' so bad, you know. Everybody know how he does make the living; but he would starve rather than see me go without. Your kind not so fussy."

The informer came back with a bottle of drink.

"Don't let these people frighten you," said the mother, waving to the score or so persons round them. "There in't a honest one here, praise the Lord. You know where you stand with them. Drink up, ne?"

Galton put the bottle to his lips and drank most of it before he stopped and wiped his mouth.

"What're you celebrating?" Galton asked.

"He din' tell you?" asked the mother with some surprise. "I thought he say you was good friends. He get some money from the police. Money and liquor. . . . Corrie! Come here!"

Another middle-aged woman approached, heavily made up in powder and lipstick.

"That's me sister, Galton. I only see she when money around."

Her sister flounced away without greeting Galton.

"What you doing in this tenement, Galton?" asked the informer's mother.

"Living, like everybody else," he replied.

"Why you don't talk, eh?"

"I don't have anything to say, I suppose," Galton answered.

"My husband never use to talk either. He use to come in, eat his food and just sit down. But he in' got your eyes."

She took his hands in her and began rubbing them.

"You married?"

"Yes," Galton answered.

"You must get a lot of children. Is like insurance, you know. You girl children going like you. I can tell. But not you boy children. People expect too much of their children. Not me! I don't expect nothing and I don't get nothing, except from him. You know, one of my children is a clerk. But if he see me 'pon the road he start complaining that he pockets empty, even though I din' ask he for nothing. Is he conscience. He wife got one pair of drawers and she got to stay home when she wash it. That's children for you."

"Is what you telling my neighbour, eh?" asked the informer, who had come over and was standing by his mother.

"Nothing! You go on 'bout you business," his mother ordered.

When he rejoined his friends she said, "Pity he's a batty-man. You din' know? You don't know a lot, Galton. You ever see he in the company of a young woman? He only like men. Is disgusting, but he's me son. There in't got one batty-man in my family, or in my husband own. I in' know where he pick up the germ from. Look at them! All men, excepting for me sister. Is where you wife?"

"Upstairs," Galton answered.

"And whey you coming from at this time, eh?" she asked, nudging him in his ribs. "You men with the innocent look who ready for anything. I know all you! A quickie behind the paling and you come out with you head high in the air as if nothing happen. Ah, men! My husband was a tiger in his house, wouldn't even laugh with his children; and one day when I go down to the Customs whey he was a messenger this tiger with the long teeth was a lil mouse. Yes! When the man say, 'Artrum! Come here!' my tiger husband jump up and shout, 'Yes, sir!' I tell you he shoot across the corridor like grease lightning."

Galton was put out by the woman's honest talk. He wished to get up and say good night, but her extraordinary presence kept him riveted to his seat. The informer seemed to be afraid of her and her sister had not answered her when she was insulted.

"I don't like domineering women," Galton said to her.

"Why you tell me that?" she asked. "You sit here so quiet while I talk, and all the time you sizing me up. Well, I never!"

She took his hand and started to laugh.

"You right, you know," she said, "I domin . . . whatever you call me."

With that the informer's mother kissed him on his lips again. Galton recoiled in disgust.

"If you come home with me," she whispered, "I can show you what you wife can never know."

"You're a . . ." began Galton, appalled at the thought that he was in the company of a whore.

"You all right, Galton?" asked the mother, perturbed at his expression.

"Yes, I'm all right. I've got to go."

"Already?" she asked, taking both his hands.

"You going?" the informer said, on seeing him get up.

"Yes, I didn't tell my wife I'd be coming late."

The informer's mother accompanied him to the door, which she closed once they were outside.

"Goodnight," said Galton, turning to go.

She thrust her hand in her bodice and exposed her left breast.

"Touch it," she whispered. "Go on! Nobody looking. How dark it is!"

Galton stood as if mesmerised by the flabby breast.

"Go on, I say," she urged him, coming closer. "What you do to me you can do to you wife afterwards."

She drew Galton's head down with her right hand until his face was almost touching her breast.

"Go on, sweetheart. It use to be so round, one time, and hard like a star-apple; but time, you know. Time mek it like this. But is still something there, in' it? 'Cause I sure you wife. . . ."

Galton wrenched himself free and ran up the stairs.

"Why he gone so sudden?" asked the informer's mother, back inside.

"He din' even want to come in! He never come in before," answered her son.

Galton stopped on the way up the stairs, pressed his trousers and adjusted his shirt as if he had been involved in a scuffle.

When he was in the room he could not face Gemma.

"Why're you so late?" she asked.

"Downstairs, in the informer's flat."

Then he told her everything, except that the informer's mother had held his hands and exposed her breast.

"She's a whore," he said.

"One of them lived down the street not far from us in Wismar," Gemma told him. "She only took in teachers. Sometimes she used to entertain them together, cook for them and give them drinks. A lot of decent men used to go there. She was always well-dressed and if you saw her on the road you'd take her for a civil servant's wife."

"How you can talk of it as if nothing was wrong?" Galton asked.

"There are women like that, Galton," Gemma replied.

"I know. What you take me for, a child?"

"Don't lose your temper about such a thing."

"You call that a little thing? Selling your body?"

Gemma, reluctant to rouse him, did not answer.

"Is it a little thing then?" he asked again.

"Please don't let us quarrel," she pleaded.

She took his hands just as the informer's mother had done, but with a violent jerk he pulled them away.

"So!" he exclaimed. And then, speaking softly, almost in a whisper, repeated: "So."

"What did I do?" she asked, for the first time afraid of him.

"Downstairs, that's how she did take my hands and rub them in hers and laugh . . . an old woman like that. 'A lot of decent men used to go there'? What's that you say? Which decent man would go with a woman like that, after she'd soiled and re-soiled herself and taken money into the bargain for steeping herself in filth?"

Gemma stared at him, dumbfounded. Only the night before he had been laughing and joking with the watchman, who came frequently to see him.

"You can stand there," Galton continued, "and talk of whores and decent men, when you came into marriage under false pretences! I should've done it, since I was a boy, snuffed this thing before it grew fat."

He accompanied this last remark by tapping his right temple with the middle finger of his right hand. Gemma stood with her head bowed, bewildered by the suddenness and violence of her husband's outburst. He was talking like some of the inhabitants of the tenement all because of one remark she had made!

When he fell into a brooding silence she warmed up his food and sat at table to show him that she bore no ill will. Galton could not get over the extraordinary coincidence of the way both his wife and the informer's mother had taken his hands in theirs. At the same time Gemma was reflecting on the informer's fatal attraction for her husband

and his indirect influence on their lives. She believed that a friendlier attitude towards him might alter things, but she only had to set eyes on him to be filled with such revulsion as to make her all the more determined to avoid him.

Galton was as ashamed at his conduct downstairs as he was angry with Gemma. He could not get over his hesitation in fleeing when the informer's mother took out her breast. The mere thought of the incident put him in a state of fury, so that Gemma, noticing his agitation, was prepared for another outburst.

Besides, the informer's mother had hit the mark when she suggested that relations between himself and Gemma were not what they ought to be. Not once had he fondled Gemma's breast, in the belief that he would be engaging in an abnormal practice. The informer's mother had never met him before, and yet she had been capable of exposing his condition so cruelly. Was it like that with others with whom he came into contact? Did the watchman understand him so well? Sometimes his heart was filled with such murderous hatred towards women he dreaded the long hours by his wife's side.

FOURTEEN

There was a knock on the door. When Gemma opened she saw the watchman and was relieved to have company. In the weeks they had been living there a close friendship had developed between him and the young couple, fed by that curious attraction that, in certain circumstances, binds people together in a very short time.

"Galton's gone to classes," she said.

"I know; I promised to get him some Rupununi tobacco."

He gave her the packet of tobacco.

"Wha' wrong?" he asked.

"It's the man downstairs. Sit down, ne," suggested Gemma, and herself took a seat.

He did likewise, taking off his cap, which he placed on the table, its shiny lining reflecting the light from the electric bulb.

"He come up?" asked the watchman.

"No, but a man came to see me yesterday and I think he saw him."

"In the day?"

"Yes," she answered. "I stayed home from work. I thought I heard someone on the landing, but I didn't go and look."

"I don't understand," said the watchman.

The urge to confide in him was so strong she yielded to it before she could decide whether she ought to trust him or not.

"This man's a friend of my father's. He came to see me as he was in Georgetown."

"What wrong with that?" asked the watchman.

"Galton's so jealous, I don't know," she said.

"If it was only a visit he in' got nothing to be jealous 'bout."

"You don't know Galton. I hope you don't go and tell him," she said.

The watchman disdained to say anything.

"The man's old enough to be my father," Gemma went on. "But you don't know Galton. I've only got him and he doesn't understand."

She went on to talk of their experiences at Winston's house. The watchman did not recognise the Galton he knew in the incidents described, but he betrayed no surprise, allowing her to speak without interruption. When, at length, she finished, he got up and was about to go, but she restrained him.

"Look!" he said, almost angrily. "If you going leave him it might be better you lef him now, y'know."

"Leave him?" she asked. "You're mad?"

"Who's this man? This friend of you father?"

"I knew him since I was a girl. He. . . . I can't tell you any more except he's a friend of my father's."

"And how he come just the day when you stay home from work?" enquired the watchman.

"It just happened, I swear it. I asked him to come because I don't know what to do."

The watchman lit a cigarette and sat down again.

"In't things getting better?" he asked. "Galton tell me he want to open a radio shop. In the end you-all going get you own house and. . . ."

"He doesn't want that!" exclaimed Gemma, interrupting him with unexpected force.

"But he tell me so. You think he want to live here all his life and bring up his children here?"

Gemma got up and lit a tiny kerosene stove Galton had bought her since they moved into the tenement.

"You want some coffee?" she asked the watchman.

He nodded.

"My brother been abroad," he declared, "for twenty-four years; and when he come back he din' know my sister name. Yes, Galton wife, he din' even remember she name. My sister wouldn't talk to him after that and he couldn't understand. People got pride and is no use saying wasn't you fault. You kian' go 'bout calling people by somebody else name. How much more when you deliberately insult you husband by sending for another man to come and see you? If you not happy why not go home and lef' him before he kian' do without you, eh?"

"I can't do that," replied Gemma.

The watchman sighed.

"Galton wife," he said, "I don't understand you. I mean, why you still see this man? This man from Wismar. You couldn't write him if you was so unhappy? And why you do it just when Galton getting somewhere wit' his studies?"

Gemma stared at him and he felt that he had gone too far.

"Because I've got a child by him," she said.

The watchman, stunned into silence, immediately thought of Galton. His young friend's undemonstrative generosity had so impressed him that he often wished that the occasion to do him a service in return would present itself.

"I didn't tell Galton," said Gemma, "because I knew he wouldn't marry me. Pa was ashamed I wasn't married and he wanted Galton to come back to Wismar and marry me. The child's with his father—Pa didn't want it in the house. Even before I had the child, when Galton came to live with me. Pa got an old lady to put something in Galton's food to make him marry me, but it didn't work. The way Pa felt he could've chained Galton and kept him there. I used to dread the nights. There was only the radio and books. . . ."

"That's education!" exclaimed the watchman. "It addle you brains and mek you long for things you don't need. All-you dream of talking good and buying electric toasters and coming to Georgetown. Of all the people I know I respect Galton most. Y'know why? 'Cause he sensitive enough to be frighten! He heself tell me that when he see the electric toaster 'pon the bed in between all them wedding presents he start trimbling and he din' know why. If we had any sense we would crucify people that invent them things!"

Gemma, believing that he had missed the point of her disclosure, was put out that he should go on about electric toasters now. She blew out the flame and poured the boiling water into their respective cups. Then, after adding two spoonfuls of brown sugar to each cup, she placed one on the table beside the watchman.

When she saw him raise the cup to his mouth she remembered a remark her father once made:

"I don't understand why you don't like young men."

From that moment she became aware that her attitude to young men was in striking contrast to that of other girls. On the rare occasions that they came to their house she either ignored them or disparaged their speech or their behaviour. Galton was the first one to whom she had been attracted, and, in retrospect, it must have been on account of his connection with Georgetown.

"If I was you I would tell Galton," advised the watchman. "The neighbour mus'a listen to you and the man talking from behind the door. He going come back again, Galton wife. I telling you. He going come back again."

The watchman got up once more and, without another word, opened the door and went out, while Gemma watched him from the landing. For the first time she noticed that he walked with a slight limp.

She went back into the room that lacked bed, dressers, cupboards, running water and the many other conveniences associated with a home.

While she waited for Galton to come home, Gemma weighed up the arguments for and against telling him about the visit from the family friend from Wismar. There was no certainty that the neighbour knew anything. Besides, if he did, she could deny whatever he said. After all, Galton knew that he was an informer. But this was the wrong time to raise doubts in her husband's mind. He had almost forgotten about their stay in Winston's house and even spoke of going to look him up when he had time. Yet, the same doubts would be raised by her confession that she had had the visit, especially as she had not told him that she was not going to work; this alone would lead him to suspect that she had been expecting the visit. In the circumstances, it was best to say nothing.

Everything seemed to be happening at once. Her father had written that he wanted to sell the shop and come to Georgetown; and tomorrow she would have to go and see the doctor to find out if she was pregnant.

A cold shiver ran over her body when it occurred to her that the watchman might relay to Galton everything she had told him. It was foolish in the extreme to confide in him. However tight-lipped he was he might inform Galton of their conversation, as an act of self-defence, fearing that she might do so first.

At the sound of footsteps on the stairs Gemma sat up, expecting Galton to come in, but the person went up to the floor above. Although the house had two storeys the pillars on which it rested had been enclosed, so as to provide an extra flat, where the informer lived. His was the only self-contained accommodation, as the outside staircase led directly to Galton's floor. When, several minutes later, she heard what was unmistakably Galton's voice she feared the worst; but whoever had engaged him in conversation did not keep him long.

"How did it go tonight?" she asked him.

"All right," he answered. "The man downstairs just put his head out to say goodnight, but I didn't feel like talking. He sounded as if he wanted to tell me something."

"I know what it is," said Gemma, unable to bear the suspense any longer. "It was because somebody came to see me a week or so ago. A man from Wismar."

"Why you didn't tell me? A friend of your father's?"

"Yes. Pa wrote that he was coming to look me up and I stayed home to see him."

A shadow passed over Galton's face.

"I know how you take the least thing to mean something, so I didn't bother to say anything," she added.

"He's gone back to Wismar?"

"Yes, the same day. He came. . . ."

"Was it the same man who—"

"No," she answered, "not him. You see why I didn't tell you. You're suspicious of everybody."

Galton smiled and Gemma despised him for believing her so readily. Experience had taught her the necessity of dissembling. If soon after their marriage she had discovered less than a hero in him, as time passed he displayed most of the weaknesses of the young men with whom she had come into contact.

That night she gave herself to Galton in a manner that flattered him to such a degree that he looked on it as the real consummation of their marriage. Afterwards, she did not put back on her pants and he did not mind.

FIFTEEN

The neighbour watched for the first opportunity to see Galton on his own, and when, that afternoon, Gemma went to the doctor he knocked on the door.

"Is the sugar; I come to bring it back."

Galton had no intention of letting him in.

"I want t'ask you advice 'bout something, Mr Flood. Is 'bout me mother," he declared.

Galton opened the door and said, "Go on, I'm listening."

"You don't happen to have a lil cotton seed oil, eh? She been groaning all morning and. . . ."

As Galton was walking over to the table where the tins and bottles were kept the neighbour slipped in and closed the door behind him.

"She don't usually stay with me, but me sister gone to tek part in one of them self-help schemes. She's a big government supporter, she and me mother. You dare not open you mouth and say nothing 'bout the government or she down you throat in labba time."

Galton gave him a bottle with some oil in the bottom of it and said, "Here's the oil. Now go and don't come back here, please."

"That's one thing you mustn't do, Mr Flood, throw a man out. I'm you guest and I did come. . . ."

Galton grabbed hold of his arm and tried to lead him to the door.

"I understand you wife treating me like a dog, but not you, Mr Flood. If it wasn't for she you would let me in. You only spurn me in you own place—but is because of she. You ask she what a man does come hey for every Wednesday, then. Ah!" exclaimed the neighbour, when he felt the pressure on his arm decrease. "Ah! that wake you up, eh? Jealousy's a terrible thing, eh? Terrible, Mr Flood. Every emotion got a value, excep' jealousy. And when it creep in you house it don't go 'way. My name is Harris; me mother name is Warren and me father was Mr Errol. You know, Mr Flood, the jealousy get knock out of me since I was a boy. I see in our bed me father, the landlord and the man me mother work for. Me mother is a real socialist, that's why she likes this government."

"My wife's been going to work every day," said Galton hopefully.

"If you say so, Mr Flood. But I home in the daytime and I hear all the noises in the house, the whispering, the groaning, the women crying 'cause their husbands don't give them enough money. Y'know, if it was for me I would let women run the country. They do things in a big way—they got vision! Is a funny thing, whenever I get in a conversation I does steer it to women. I don't know why. Is like a obsession. Women, they got what men in' got: patience, a deep, voiceless patience; but when they strike! Oh, me God! Is like the floods every ten years that does cover the coast from Rossignol to Parika and lef' a trail of dead cattle in it wake. You see, I not ignorant. I know something 'bout life. I even help deliver a baby one time. When I think of the way my mother suffer I does want to lash out with a hatchet at all these self-satisfied people galloping to the stores! I got about twenty aunts and when I was a boy I was proud to tramp from one house to the other listening to their talk. They all did like me. Yes, as a boy some people did like me bad. I was kind, they did say; but if they did know the filth that lurk in me, just waiting for the first 'portunity to break out they would 'a lock their doors when they see me coming. Instinct is a funny thing; they know I couldn't do them nothing. Not in the daytime at least. Is night when all them crawling things in me head wake up and. . . ."

"If what you say about my wife isn't true," observed Galton calmly, "I'll kill you."

For the first time the neighbour betrayed uneasiness. Galton went over to the table and picked up an armful of the tins, packets and bottles and offered them to the neighbour, who did not know what to do.

"I din' tell you for this!" he said, edging towards the door.

"Take it!" Galton ordered him.

Carefully he took the pile of things from Galton and as the latter freed himself of the armful the tin of sugar fell to the floor. Its lid came off and its contents were spilled over the centre of the room.

"Doesn't matter, doesn't matter," Galton said, opening the door. He then closed it and felt the blood drain from his head. He was not able to live like this any longer. Before he could collect his thoughts the door opened and his wife walked in.

"What's that on the floor?" she asked.

"Sugar, Gemma. Sugar. Get the broom and sweep it up."

Seeing that something was amiss she obeyed quietly. When she had finished and had put away the broom he declared:

"The neighbour told me about your Wednesday visits."

"Visits? He came once!" she protested.

"I don't believe you," said Galton, with a chilling calm.

"I had one visit. You don't have to believe me, but he came once."

"He's been coming every Wednesday," Galton insisted.

"But I've got my pay-slips. You can see for yourself how many times I've been absent."

Galton reflected that she might be telling the truth, but could not resist saying, "Your idea of marriage and mine aren't the same. You wouldn't have told me about the visit if you weren't afraid of the man downstairs. How do I know there aren't other things you haven't told me?"

Galton wondered at her silence.

"All you should expect of me is that I should work as hard as you," she said after a while. "I don't expect more of you."

He could not believe his ears. "You're defying me?"

"Before you married me I was free, Galton. I think we could make a go of our marriage, but I'm not giving up my freedom."

Galton made a heroic effort not to lose his self-control.

"You trapped me by writing passionate letters and now have the gall to tell me you want your independence? Your attitude since we moved to this house's been one of continual defiance. The more you have to answer for the more you—"

She interrupted him, raising her voice, "I have *nothing* to answer for. There *are* things in the past I haven't told you, but since we've been married I've hidden nothing from you except the *one* visit from this man. And I'll tell you, if you hadn't brought me to live here I wouldn't have dreamed of asking for his help. Yes, I sent for him to ask for his help. I couldn't live like this any more. Even *you* can't sleep at night because of the noises and the banging on doors. Every morning you get up around three and you can't fall asleep again."

"It's not the noises that wake me," he countered.

"What then?" she asked.

"I don't know. I only know it's not the noises. . . . If we don't separate. . . ."

"Very well, Galton, we'll separate," she declared, as if she had anticipated the suggestion.

Galton appeared to be more deeply affected by his own decision than Gemma was. The world seemed a desperately lonely place. He had hoped that the mention of separation would have caused her to regret what she had said about independence.

When Galton left the room, ostensibly to go to Selwyn's house. Gemma lay down on the mattress and wept. If only he knew how near she had come to begging him to let them start once more. She had already resolved never to invite her visitor from Wismar again.

The watchman had warned them both about the neighbour downstairs.

"I wouldn't live near to him for all the tea in China," he was wont to say. Yet Galton had listened to him and had believed him. He even used to greet him on the stairs, almost as an encouragement, it seemed to her.

In Linden they could have had a peaceful life, built a house and raised many children where there was light and space.

The night before her departure for Georgetown her father had thrown a party for her. It was attended by his cronies and their neighbours in the main, with a sprinkling of young people. *He* was there, pretending not to notice her; but she knew how he was suffering by the way he laughed.

This was the happiest day of her life, the eve of her departure from her prison. Since childhood she had watched that river, winding through their lives, and the bauxite ships becoming specks in the distance. The man-made dunes at Wismar and the river were for her symbols of her imprisonment itself. No man had offended her as Galton had: she was obliged to work among women whose conversation was mostly about men and the cinema; she was made to live in a room less attractive than the dog's under her father's house. But how could she go back to Wismar so soon after the party, the goodbyes, the wedding presents, the good wishes and expressions of envy at her good fortune. There was nowhere to hide in that small community. She could imagine people calling out, "You back? So soon?" without a trace of malice.

Gemma had not bothered to tell Galton that the doctor believed she was expecting. In a few days the tests would probably confirm his diagnosis and she would have to decide whether or not she should get rid of it. The midwife at Wismar once said that many of the women who allowed their bodies to be tampered with had to undergo operations in their forties. It seemed to her that so often one was forced to choose between one's pride and one's interests. It was in her interest to let the seed in her grow, yea, in the face of her offended pride, even though people would be only too willing to believe that she was not even married, that she had left Wismar to live with a man whom she could not keep for more than a few months.

The same night a child was born in the tenement. The screams of the woman in labour came through the floorboards and resounded in their room; and when the alarm clock rang at half-past six Galton was so fast asleep he did not hear it. On waking, a little after eight, he found that Gemma had gone to work.

He remained in bed all day and only got up to go down to the toilet. As thoughts raced through his mind all sorts of imaginary problems presented themselves, demanding an urgent solution. At one point he was haunted by an idea that had obsessed him for several days after his mother's death: the belief that her body had not been buried. He got up, lifted the mattress, and, finding nothing there, went to the window, where he stood staring down at the alleyway, which was bathed in sunshine. Without bothering to change he ran downstairs as if his life depended on it. He pushed aside a paling-stave that had come loose at the bottom, then slipped into the alleyway.

Close against the fence on the other side was the branch of a ginnip tree, apparently cut and discarded a few days before. Its leaves had become brown and brittle and only here and there could patches of green be seen. Stepping over the gutter Galton bent down slowly. His eyes staring, he suddenly hoisted the branch in the air, revealing nothing but grey earth. He returned trembling to the room and lay down again. And all day long he lay on the mattress, his head aching with thoughts and desires. Of a sudden he burst out laughing; he had recalled a Yoruba proverb which purported to define humanity between heaven and earth: "A pile of shit on a leaf covered by a leaf." He laughed there, lying on his back, until the tears came; he laughed as heartily as his wife had wept bitterly the night before.

Lately Galton imagined that Gemma's feelings for him were something less than love. However, he was not sure and kept telling himself that things must be so in marriage: that it was seemly for a wife to be undemonstrative. But the startling confirmation of a waning affection came with her demand to be independent. Independent! Was he independent of her? For him the essential term of marriage could only be the complete subservience of the woman. He had been unwilling to marry because he could never endure a failure as his father had. Now he was so far! Before him lay only ghost-like moon shadows between houses of a deserted road and the eyes behind the lattice-work. He had walked that road a hundred times in his dreams, but only once had found anyone waiting at the end of it: his mother, dressed in mauve.

Overcome by a feeling of elation Galton got up, took a shower in the bathroom in the yard and went out just before Gemma came home. When he returned after ten that night he found her waiting for him in a state of great agitation.

"Where've you been?" she asked.

"Nowhere. Been walking about for a bit and to see the watchman."

Gemma poured his chocolate back into the pan to warm it up again. She had been worrying lest he might have done something rash.

"You're still vexed?" she asked.

"No, no. What for?"

While he was eating he suggested that they go to Pouderoyen by launch. He wanted to see someone who was looking for a partner in his radio shop.

"Pa can lend you some money," she said eagerly.

"Can he?"

"Yes."

"We've got to hurry, though," he said, swallowing the chocolate in gulps.

"What? It's tonight?"

"Yes. I agreed we'd leave by eleven," said Galton.

Gemma looked at him suspiciously.

"You don't have to go if you don't want to," he said, wiping his mouth.

Galton got up, buttoning up his shirt as he did so.

"All right, I'm coming," she said and got up as well.

He hurried on ahead of her and she was obliged to run to catch up with him in the passage.

He reflected that he would have been more content if she had shown less interest in his welfare. When he returned home she was obviously worried. His mother used to be especially pleasant to his father whenever she wanted something from him. Even as a very small boy he saw through the ruse; but his father never failed to fall victim to her wiles. Gemma was cast in the same mould as his mother.

Where've you been? were her words. "Where've you been?" he said to himself. "You'll find out where I've been, you Wismar rat!"

Gemma hurried along by his side.

"Why're you hurrying so?" she asked.

"To get there in time."

His anger redoubled at the sound of her voice.

"All right, I'll slow down," he said, feigning gentleness.

At that, she thrust her arm under his. As they approached the passage next to the market, which led to the wharf, he increased his pace imperceptibly.

They stood at the head of the ramp that served as a wharf for the launches which made the journey from Pouderoyen, laden with vegetables for market and people making the occasional trip to Georgetown from the West Bank.

The flood tide was lapping at the lower beams that spanned the greenheart piles.

"It's cold," complained Gemma.

"The boat should be coming any time now," Galton reassured her.

"But I can't see any lights," she remarked, looking at him.

"Wait here," said Galton, "I'm going down to see."

He carefully descended the ramp, which was rising and falling with the water. From a recess on the left he drew a piece of wood. Bending forward and looking across the river to the left he said, "I can see it! Come down."

Gemma descended the ramp sideways to reduce the risk of slipping, and on reaching the bottom she held on to him.

"Come on this side, you'll see the lights," suggested Galton.

He stepped back to allow her to cross to his left side and as she hesitated he lifted the length of wood and brought it down on her head with a thud, whereupon all the repressed anger of his boyhood came flooding out like water through a breached koker. She stood, immobile, for a second, raised her hand to her head and swayed before the second blow felled her, face down in the water. Galton jumped after her and pulled her towards the ramp, where, with great difficulty, he managed to drag her on to it. He took out a length of chain, from the recess, where he had hidden the wood, to which four lead weights had been attached by bits of wire.

Galton looked round to make certain that he was not being observed, but nothing moved; and the street, which he could only see when the ramp rose to its highest point, kept appearing and disappearing at intervals. For a split second he came into the view of anyone who might have happened to be passing.

He worked as quickly as was prudent and when, at the end of what seemed an eternity, he eased Gemma's head into the water, the body sank, dragged downwards by the weights round its neck. She must have been still breathing for a pair of bubbles rose to the surface, seconds after the body had disappeared in the murky water.

Galton turned to go and then, as an afterthought, picked up the length of greenheart and threw it into the river.

When it was all over he realised how hungry he was. The one meal he had eaten that day had not satisfied him.

Back in Lombard Street he entered the cook-shop and ordered curry-beef and a cuttie of rum. In the corner three men were drinking.

"He been tekking home he money to he mother, even after he get marry! A big man like he," one of the men said.

"Some men like that," put in a second. "And they expect the woman to put up with it. I mean, fair's fair. But you in' hear nothing yet. My father always telling his friend 'bout the time me mother threaten to go home to she father and complain how he beating she. 'Go, ne!' me father say to she. 'Go and bring he and I going give he licks heself.' And me mother go to she father and show he the bruises 'pon she hip. By this time me father was squaring up at home waiting for he father-in-law to come. When he see them coming down the road he open the door and tek off he belt. Me grandfather drag me mother up the stairs and in the house. 'Archie!' he say to me father, 'you beat a woman and only give she two bruise 'pon she hip! Well, I going show you how for do it!' And me grandfather start belabouring me mother like a estate mule. Pie! Pie!" And the young man flicked his right hand through the air, causing his fingers to produce the sound of a whip.

All three men roared with laughter at the young man's mother's plight.

It was unbelievable that people could be joking at a time like this, Galton thought.

"You story show how man tchupid," said the third man, nodding towards one of the men. "And you story show how woman tchupid," he declared, nodding towards the other. "But me story going show how man *and* woman tchupid together. This man and this woman get married

and none of them did know how for do it. So they go to
the village elder and ask he what they got to do for get
children. Three year did pass and they din' do it yet. Eh,
eh! The village elder tell them to come back next night at
eleven o'clock when everybody was asleep and that the
woman had to cover she nakedness with a white dress.
By rights she should be naked, he say, but he was a man
of great modesty. Woman nakedness was for woman and
man nakedness was for man. Eh, eh! The next night come
and the man tek he wife back to the elder house, wearing
a long white dress. The husband insist that the dress had
to be long, 'cause the elder was a modest man and din'
like woman nakedness. When they reach the elder house
he talk to them and give them white rum, and when the
man was proper drunk he send he out to the backdam
to kneel down and pray under the jamoon tree. So the
man go and pray as he was told; and when he come back
the elder tell he that he wife been visited by the Holy
Ghost. . . ."

At this the two listeners could no longer contain their
amusement. One of them threw himself into the air and
fell back on to the bench, while the other writhed like a
comoodie on the side of the table.

"Eh, eh! Oh, me God!" exclaimed the one who was
squirming on the bench. "Me side hurting me. Stop, man,
stop!"

"Anyway," continued the man telling the story, "the
man look 'pon he wife and say, 'The Holy Ghost! What
he look like?'"

The outburst of laughter that greeted this question
caused two passers-by to stop and look in. They themselves

began laughing and remained to hear what was the cause of the mirth.

"'He got—' the wife start saying. But the elder get vex and tell the man, 'You never ask a question like that, or else you wife won't bear no children.' The man and woman go home. Eh, eh! On the way home she start showing she teeth and talking a lot and she husband say, 'Is why you so happy for?' And she say, 'I feel so nice and happy. And when I get home I going show you the Virgin Mary!'"

The owner of the cook-shop shouted out at the men, who were by this time screaming with delight.

"You want to wake the whole town? Is what wrong wit' you at all?"

When Galton left, distressed by the mirth, he did not want to go back to his room. Instead, he slept at the watchman's sawmill and went home in the morning.

The same night the watchman came to see him. His day-shift had begun that day. Galton told him that Gemma had gone back to Wismar.

"When?"

"Yesterday," Galton answered.

"I thought something was funny wit' you last night," observed the watchman. "Why you din' say nothing?"

Galton did not reply. After a few moments he said, "You think I'm grieved. Now it's come to it . . . now I don't even know what I feel. . . . This room's dark."

"It was always dark," observed the watchman, who was inwardly blaming himself for having given Gemma the advice to leave Galton before it was too late. He was convinced that she had taken him seriously and left his friend.

"Now, at this moment," Galton said, standing in the middle of the room, "at this *particular* moment in time," and he gave the word "particular" great emphasis, "you can't know what I miss most of all: her dresses hanging on the nail behind the door. It's not even conceivable that I miss her dresses more than . . . pieces of cloth with buttons down the middle, and the smell of sweat on them. That's what I miss most of all of the seven infernal months in this room. Last year I saw a friend I went to school with. I thought he was abroad. I went up to him and said, 'Rennie,' and he pulled away from me as if he didn't know me. In the couple of years I hadn't seen him he'd gone off his head. He'd taken to roaming the streets. It was. . . . She liked to write me perfumed letters, you know, and send them in envelopes with lining that made a crackling sound when you opened them. . . . Here, I'm talking like a woman because my wife gone to Linden. You know the new road to Linden?"

The watchman nodded.

"It's straight as a die. How man can build anything straight I'll never know, because . . . because . . . 'The water at Peter's Hall discoloured the cups.' A strange thing to say at that time."

Suddenly Galton grasped the watchman's hand.

"What if your wife said that the water at Peter's Hall discoloured the cups? Eh? Because, you see, it did. It was a kind of scum that discoloured the crockery and would not come off. But!"

He was now speaking very quickly.

"But! And here you've got to hand it to the government: they're extending the pure water supply scheme to the East Bank and so the water will not discolour the cups. How about that then, eh? The government acts and . . . no scum!"

Galton let go of his friend, who had made no effort to shake himself free. He stood looking at him and then, after a while, went and sat down in one of the two chairs at the table.

"Did you know," continued Galton, "that about three days before a human being dies he becomes deaf for a short while—from a few minutes to a few hours—and during that time he hears loud, sometimes unbearable music. Usually, he rallies after that and thinks he's got a new lease of life. In fact the hammer's already fallen and smashed his life; but to the end, we've got to lie to ourselves; and nature's only too happy to oblige. You see that alley through the window," Galton said, pointing out of the window, "that's the most interesting place in this town. At night you see a whole procession of our people passing there: couples making love, men pissing against the palings, children hiding from their parents, escapees from the police scaling the zinc, furtive rubbish dumpers. Gemma used to complain that you couldn't see anything through the window, not even a tree. But women're afraid of what they see: it reminds them of too much. . . . That man downstairs, the neighbour, the one you call the informer. I like him because he's so vile you know you'll soil your hands when you touch him. But that vile police informer cries when he can't find money to give his mother. Need I say more?"

The watchman did not take his gaze away from him for a single moment.

"I could tell you a lot that would sicken you, only because it's true. . . . I met a man who wanted to scandalise the people in a cake shop. He said that Judas was his hero. And no sooner were the words out of his mouth than I understood. Judas's conscience tormented him so, he hanged himself. He is the only character in the Bible who couldn't lie to himself. . . . I've been lying to myself since . . . since . . . about my mother, my father, Selwyn, Nekka, Winston. But my dreams give me away. Guyanese are a dreaming people. We have strong, sinewy dreams, like muscular lyrics, where people talk to us and tell us what to do. That's why Gemma went away. Because I never shared one dream with her. *I* can't share, you see," he declared with an expression of utter dejection. "My generosity isn't real; it's only skin deep."

He sat down on the other chair. His last words had been delivered almost in a whisper.

"I don't sleep well, you know," he said, looking up at the watchman as if he had made a confession. "I keep waking in the morning about three o'clock. Always around three o'clock. I'm not worried. It'll pass. . . ."

Galton looked down at the floor and shook his head, all the while saying, "Tch! Tch!"

"I don't know how I can love a woman who's indifferent to me," he said, looking up at the watchman once more.

The watchman got up again.

"Let's go out and walk," he suggested.

From a room on the floor above there was a fit of coughing. On closing the door behind them they heard the coughing again and looking up saw the old man on the landing.

"You Mr Flood?" he asked, doing his best to restrain himself from coughing. "A letter come hey to you. I in' know why they deliver it hey; I in' look like you."

He went back into his room and returned with the letter. Galton then climbed the stairs and took it from him.

"I in't see you for a few days," observed the old man. "You and you wife so quiet. I see nine sets of people come and go in that room. Nine," he repeated, indicating the number on his two hands. "The room cursed, I always tell my daughter. Nine sets of people, but you're the quietest."

The old man went back inside and left Galton opening his letter. It was only the electricity bill for the previous month. He stared at it and smiled wryly.

"Come on, ne," the watchman said, fearing another outburst.

Galton stopped and looked at him.

"You know you're the ugliest man I know!" exclaimed Galton. "Your fingers are short, your head's shaped like a mango and. . . ."

He stood by the watchman, unable to finish his description satisfactorily. He then put his hands in his pockets and walked behind the older man. They turned into Upper Water Street, where the sawmills were. Galton stopped.

"Where the hell we're going?" he asked.

"Haul you rass!" came the reply from the watchman, who continued on his way.

A few yards beyond the market, the latter turned into a passage which took them to a wharf. Below them the water shuddered around the massive greenheart piles. Galton hesitated for a while, then followed his friend on to a boat moored to the wharf.

"Is you?" a voice called out.

"Is me!" answered the watchman, who climbed the rest of the gang-plank and boarded the boat.

It appeared to Galton to be one of the craft that did the trip to the Pomeroon in the north-west. The deck was slippery and there was no light, but by holding on to the cables he managed to follow the watchman into the cabin, through a doorway and into another sort of cabin, which was ill lit.

The watchman introduced Galton to the captain and two men who were talking with him. The former passed the newcomers the bottle of rum, but Galton hesitated before he poured himself a tot. He then passed the bottle to the watchman, who gave himself a generous shot.

An old porknocker was recounting his experiences at Issano. Galton had heard all this before when he was in the bush, but the slight rolling of the boat, the effect of the rum—which he had not touched since the night he and Gemma left Winston's house—and the company, combined to impart a certain magic to the story.

Perhaps it was his failing that he did not have a wide enough circle of male friends. During the months he had worked as a watchman there had been opportunities to pass the time in the company of men of action, who plied the river or the coast. They were not fettered to one place and were accustomed to being drenched by the rain. The city was sucking his blood like some enormous leech, before which he stood mesmerised.

From the stories the watchman told it was obvious that he as well had worked in the bush. He explained how he had learned to cut greenheart planks with an axe; and to give conviction to his description took off the shoe of his left foot to show where he had lost a little toe during his apprenticeship.

The session reminded him of his time in the bush and the long hours of story-telling after a day's work. As the cabin became choked with cigarette smoke and the men's voices became more boisterous Galton forgot the events of the previous night. Someone went to buy black-pudding and on his return the men unceremoniously broke off bits of the rice-stuffed entrails and ate them.

"They ban sardines, but we still got black-pudding," smiled the captain.

The watchman stepped out on deck for some fresh air and, when Galton joined him, asked, "How you feel now?"

"How I feel? I need money, that's how I feel. On Friday we'll celebrate my separation and freedom."

The few lights on the river were stationary and the water, rank with the new tide, rose and sank in a gentle swell. One of the men started playing an accordion, first in tantalising fits and starts until, confident in his intention, with a sweet, haunting legato.

BOOK TWO

Only with kisses and poppies can I love you.
With rain-sodden wreaths.
As I brood on ashen horses
And the yellow of dogs.

—*Pablo Neruda*

SIXTEEN

Selwyn stopped in front of the passage which led to Galton's tenement. At the entrance, sitting on a stool which disappeared under her enormous body, was a young woman who could not have been more than twenty. She was dressed in black and on her lap was a plate with a great mound of rice and curry on it. New to the district, she was a hanger-on of the cook-shop that flanked the passage, and spent much of the day on her stool where passers-by and tenants of the tenement frequently engaged her in conversation.

"Is there a Mr Flood living at the back?" asked Selwyn.

The young woman looked up as if she did not understand.

"A Mr Flood," repeated Selwyn.

"They got a man call Galton living on the second floor that look like you, but I never hear nobody call he Flood."

"Thanks," said Selwyn, who took a decisive step into the passage. He was more apprehensive about his own safety than he appeared. Apart from the evil reputation of Lombard Street one of the two youths who were conversing in the doorway of the cook-shop had been casting furtive glances at him.

The passage was longer than he had imagined and on reaching the foot of the staircase that led up to the tenement he reflected on his chances of escaping if he were attacked. On his way up the stairs he heard someone say, "He in' there; he in' come home yet."

"You're talking to me?" asked Selwyn, who began to come back down the stairs.

"I here," said the voice.

Selwyn caught sight of the man leaning out of the window under the staircase where it turned at right angles.

"Come, mister. You can wait for he hey."

"No, thanks," retorted Selwyn. "I'll come back."

"Come in, I tell you. Is Galton friend. Without me he would'a lef' here long ago."

The neighbour had opened his door and Selwyn entered, unwilling to offend someone on whose goodwill Galton's safety might depend.

In contrast to Galton's room the neighbour's was neatly furnished with two armchairs, a well-made bed and a handsome radio-record-player console.

"Sit down here," he said, offering Selwyn one of the armchairs. He turned on the light and unhooked the blind.

"It going rain. It close bad, eh? . . . I like sitting in the dark. Is just a habit. But when I got guests I does give them all the light I got. . . . So you's Galton brother! All you resemble bad! I never see nothing so in me life! You look like twins. . . . You in' got a dollar to lend me, eh? I out of work these past few weeks and I got a mother to support."

Selwyn, furious with himself at having accepted the neighbour's invitation to go into his room, took out his wallet from his back pocket and extracted a dollar note from it.

The neighbour took it and observed, "Bad place to keep you money." He smiled, rubbing his hands.

"Some people is inconsiderate. You hear that noise coming from the top. He does play he record player when the children in the house sleeping. I call that most inconsiderate! Some people does give me a bad name, but you brother is a gentleman. He judge a man by he character, not he reputation. You want some mauby?"

"Thanks, no. When's Galton coming back?"

"Any minute now. You in' comfortable? You ever been involve with the police? Course not. People like you don't get involve with the police."

"Why d'you ask?" enquired Selwyn suspiciously.

"No offence. I *choose* my friends. Is a question I ask everybody. Your brother should never be living round here, mister. Only poor people and people who got something to hide does live round here. And you brother in' poor."

The neighbour's expression had changed completely. His smile had gone and he had the appearance of someone who was bent on committing an evil deed. He wanted to ask Selwyn for some more money, but felt that, having already relieved him of a dollar, a direct request would be unlikely to be successful. Further, it was obvious that Selwyn did not like him. He had done him nothing; in fact he had invited him into his room, a privilege few others had enjoyed.

"Everybody got something to hide," remarked the neighbour. "Tek that coughing man upstairs, he does live in a room on the same floor as Galton. But he daughter and she man does live in the room over Galton. So he does be in one room sometimes and the other at other times. Now he does sleep in the room opposite Galton, not in he daughter room. He does do all he coughing at night, right over me. One day I say to him, 'You better do you coughing in you daughter room, 'cause I fed up.' He look 'pon me 'cause I small in size as if I was a cockroach or something. He suck he teeth and walk away. The man get me blood up, 'cause is one thing I does demand, is respect. I start finding out 'bout this character and you know what that coughing man is? He been in jail! He's a jailbird! So the next time I see he I tell he to stop the coughing at night. I say, 'Mr Jailbird, you better stop that coughing or sleep upstairs!' You should'a see the man face! Since then he does treat me with respect. And me, I don't mind no more if he cough over me at night."

The neighbour looked at Selwyn closely to see what impression his words had made on him. The latter wanted to go. The neighbour's familiarity irritated him. Yet he was intrigued by the disclosures about the tenement in which his brother chose to live.

"People here frighten of me," said the neighbour, impatient with Selwyn's silence.

"Is Galton frightened of you?" asked Selwyn.

"No, he's me friend," came the answer.

At the sound of footsteps on the stairs the neighbour looked out.

"Is that flat-arsed watchman!" he exclaimed, with unexpected vehemence.

A few minutes later the watchman could be heard coming back down the stairs. He happened to look in and see Selwyn.

"That in' Galton brother?" he asked.

"Yes," answered Selwyn with alacrity.

"Galton give me a message for you," he said.

"I'm coming," said Selwyn, and nodded to the neighbour, who watched him accompany the watchman back up the stairs.

"Galton give me the key. He tell me to tell you to wait. He coming in about a hour. I'm his friend."

"His friend?" asked Selwyn skeptically.

He followed the watchman to Galton's room and stood in the doorway. Even before the former turned the light on he could sense the wretchedness of the accommodation. Then the light laid bare the pathetic furnishings of two chairs, a table and mattress. The musty scent of a badly aired room escaped through the open door.

"You're a friend of the man downstairs?" asked Selwyn.

"Who? He? That's a police informer," the watchman told him. "If I was you I wouldn't go in there again. The man's a dog," he added.

"He says he's Galton's friend."

"Sort of . . ." replied the watchman.

For a time the two men did not know what to say to each other. Galton's friend was about to offer Selwyn a cup of coffee, but thought better of it. Galton's brother might resent his presumptuousness.

"I work wit' him when he was a watchman, y'know," the watchman finally ventured.

"Oh! You're the one he used to talk about."

"Yes, is me," the watchman almost shouted with relief. "You thought I was like the chap downstairs! No, everybody frightened of him."

"So he said himself," Selwyn rejoined, smiling.

The ice had been broken.

"Galton want to come and live at you, y'know," said the watchman.

Selwyn looked at him questioningly.

"What wrong?" the watchman asked.

"He said so himself?" enquired Selwyn.

"Yes."

"I met him a few weeks ago and offered him the flat under the house, but he refused," Selwyn told him.

"That's funny. He been saying you din' want him back."

"I enclosed the bottom house specially for him when I heard that his wife had gone off. He wouldn't come any more to collect the money I used to pay him, and as the house belongs to both of us I enclosed it so he could come back. He knows."

"He's a funny chap," observed the watchman. "I keep saying, 'This is no place for you to live.' One night he say he couldn't sleep and when he put on the light he see the mattress crawling with bugs."

"He's been slandering me round town," said Selwyn. "Telling people I stole from him. All the money he didn't collect I've put in the bank. I've always dealt straight with him."

"Oh, if I did bother with the things he say 'bout me and the things he do me I wouldn't be in this room now, I can tell you that over and over."

"You live near here?" asked Selwyn.

"No, in the Ruimveldt Housing Scheme. I got six children. All of them big men and women, working."

Selwyn, to avoid having to speak, got up and opened the window. He cast one glance at the alleyway and thought, "What a hole to live in. It's a wonder he's not been murdered yet."

As if he had divined his thoughts, the watchman said, "Everybody know Galton round here. He don't talk much, but people know he not playing great."

Selwyn found it hard to believe that his brother had lived in such squalor for more than a year. And according to the watchman he had got to like it. If their parents were alive they would be sick with grief to see where he was staying and who his friends were. The young woman in black at the entrance consuming her curry in public summed up for Selwyn the character of the tenement and the neighbourhood. No wonder Gemma left him! Which decent woman would spend a night in a place like this?

Someone in a room on the same floor was taken with a fit of coughing.

"Is the old man," said the watchman. "It must be six o'clock."

Selwyn looked at his watch, which said two minutes past six.

"He does begin as soon as the sun go down," added the watchman.

The thought that the old man might be suffering from tuberculosis, the one disease capable of striking terror in the hearts of Guyanese, caused Selwyn to ask nervously: "He got consumption?"

"Nobody know. He kian' afford to go to the doctor, I suppose. Or he might be just frighten."

Selwyn was more determined than ever to rescue Galton from the tenement if it was in his power to do so. The noises grew in intensity with nightfall. Children were coming in from their play in the yard and on the pavement; the men were returning home from work and the women, tired after a day's labour, shouted in exasperation at the least misdemeanour on the part of those around them.

"What's the best way to get him to leave?" Selwyn asked, ashamed that he had to ask a stranger how to tackle his own brother.

"Ask he! After telling me you don't want he back he kian' refuse if you ask he in front of me," suggested the watchman.

Selwyn began to tap the floorboard with his well-shod right foot. What a far cry Lombard Street was from Kitty's wide expanses. At nightfall the six o'clock bee and the whistling frogs vied with one another and in the daytime there was no need to look over one's shoulder. He was already thinking of the moment when he would have to make his way through the dark passage to the street and walk to his car, which he had left in High Street.

His musings were interrupted by the door opening and Galton appearing in the doorway.

"At last!" exclaimed Selwyn. "I thought you'd never come."

"You got my message?" Galton asked.

"Yes, but I didn't expect you to take so long."

Galton had apparently eaten, for he did not seem disposed to prepare anything.

"I'm so tired I can go to sleep now," he announced, throwing himself down on the mattress. "I hope you-all been getting on," he remarked.

"You din' think we been waiting 'pon you to start talking," asked the watchman sarcastically, remembering the lies Galton had told him about his brother. Selwyn was surprised that Galton allowed himself to be addressed in this manner.

"You better talk to him," suggested the watchman to Selwyn, "Else he go'n fall asleep and then it'll tek more than you and me to wake he. I know what I telling you."

"What're you talking about?" Galton asked, having closed his eyes.

"You know why I came," Selwyn began. "It's about your taking the bottom house flat."

Galton opened his eyes. He closed them again and began to speak.

"Once I missed that place so bad I used to wake up in the night thinking about it. But, nothing lasts for ever. It's a place like any other place."

"You going or not?" asked the watchman brutally. "You can fool he with all that talk, not me. Just tell he if you going."

Galton sat up.

"He's right. I've got to consider it. I can't talk plainly like him."

"Don't mess me around, Galton. You're taking it or not?" asked Selwyn.

"And if I don't, what're you going to do?" enquired Galton.

"Let it, of course," came the reply. "It's a whole flat."

"I don't know why he poochpanching, mister. He want somebody to drag he from hey to Kitty!" said the watchman, becoming more and more agitated.

Although there was no doubt that the watchman had some influence on his brother, Selwyn was loath to admit that he could persuade Galton to do what he, Selwyn, could not. His brash interruptions of their conversation infuriated Selwyn, who tried to intimidate him with a look.

"Mister, one day he does cuss this place," the watchman began again, "and the next he say he kian' live nowhere else. I know that he kian' keep on living hey. He's a man got to humiliate heself. You really think he enjoy living in a room crawling with bugs? You should hear he talk when he drunk! You'd think he's the worst man upon the face of this earth! Always talking 'bout how he in' fit to live. Anybody that live near to that louse downstairs and put up with him not only fit to live but deserve to get pay. Galton's the only person in the place who *like* him."

Galton listened to all this without the slightest indication of annoyance. In fact, the watchman began to think that his friend had fallen asleep.

"Galton!" Selwyn shouted.

He opened his eyes. "Sorry, I must've dropped off," he replied.

Selwyn felt that he was entitled to ask where his brother had been to be so sleepy at that time of the evening, especially as there was little doubt that the watchman knew.

It must have begun to drizzle for there was a scent of damp through the window.

The watchman noticed Selwyn's exasperation and reflected that his impatience was likely to endanger the plan to get Galton back to his former home in Kitty. He tried to catch Selwyn's eye, but the latter stubbornly refused to look his way.

Galton was having difficulty in staying awake and when, finally, he dropped off again, neither his brother nor the watchman attempted to wake him. A pick-up upstairs was blaring out the rhythms of reggae music, which had become the rage among the youth of Georgetown. The noise of the record drowned everything else with its insistent, pulsating multiple beats.

"Where he been, to be so sleepy?" Selwyn asked the watchman.

"Nowhere. He was up late last night."

"Doing what?"

"With friends."

"Oh," said Selwyn, lifting his head slightly, as if surprised to learn that his brother had friends.

"Probably that's why he don't want to lef' hey," suggested the watchman. "He'd be far from the wharf."

"You mean he goes down to the wharves?" asked Selwyn.

"Go down, mister? He practically live here when the skipper come in with his boat."

Selwyn got up and announced that he was going.

"Stay, ne? He kian' sleep forever," the watchman urged.

"I'm married and have two children," rejoined Selwyn, maliciously. "Probably it's the best thing for him to remain. If he feels at home I don't see why he should move. He already looks like the people round here."

The watchman knew that the words were meant for him, but he had sized up Selwyn early on in their conversation and, having classified him as a "hopeless case," decided not to take offence.

The two men got up at the same time.

Selwyn's indignation at the way his meeting with Galton had gone caused him to forget his fears about going through the passageway. With firm steps he descended the staircase and strode into the dark corridor. Once on the pavement he turned right in the direction of the market and turned right again by Auto Supplies. When he arrived at his car in High Street he hesitated, thinking that he had acted too hastily in leaving his brother while he was asleep. Finally he opened the car door, got in and for a while sat without making any attempt to start the vehicle. The windscreen was blurred from the drizzle which had been falling intermittently for the last half hour. In the end the car moved off and cruised slowly along the wet pitch road, which reflected the glare of every street lamp and hissed with the passage of every vehicle. It bore right at the sea wall road, turned into Sherrif Street and drove back down Durban Street, thus circling the town. This he did once more before turning off into David Street where he lived.

Selwyn pushed the door of the new flat under the house and surveyed the front room with its newly painted walls and new electric fittings. The fact that Galton had agreed to meet him in his tenement room had led him to believe that the time was ripe for a reconciliation. He and Nekka had planned for his coming, reasoning that in a self-contained flat, doing his own cooking and relying on them for nothing Galton would not present a threat to their domestic harmony. He knew Nekka. Once the place had been let and the money began to roll in it would be more and more difficult for her to agree to give it to Galton.

Indeed, it was only the possibility that Galton might ask the court to sell the house in order to realise his share which made her amenable to Selwyn's plan for his return. She saw Galton as a thorn in their flesh and resented her husband's preoccupation with his welfare.

Selwyn sat down on an improvised work-bench left behind by the workman. The pattering of his son's feet on the floorboards could be heard distinctly. Nekka was probably feeding their baby girl, their second child.

He was puzzled by his brother's indifference. Undoubtedly the watchman was anxious that he should accept the flat, a fact which Selwyn found odd, considering that Galton would thereby be removed from his influence. Kitty was far from the wharves and even farther from Ruimveldt, where the watchman lived. Selwyn refused to believe the evidence of his own eyes, that his brother relied heavily on his friend. His allusions regarding Galton's superiority to the others in the tenement led him to the conclusion that both the watchman and the informer were preying on him and, consequently, would prefer to see him remain among them. He got up and went upstairs through the back door, which Nekka unbolted for him.

SEVENTEEN

In truth, Galton was faced with a dilemma: he could remain in the tenement, ugly and degrading, or he could return to his old home in Kitty with its barren relationships. Since that awful night, he had given up his radio course. Looking back on the nights when he had pored for hours over the involved calculations, he was astonished at the amount of work already covered. Most of his evenings were now spent chatting with the watchman at his sawmill, when he was on night duty, or drinking with the skipper when his boat was in port. But Galton knew that he could not go on living from day to day, like a stray dog. Two incidents that occurred within a few weeks after Selwyn's offer forced him to make a decision.

The first involved the coughing man, who had only recently crossed the informer in some way that was not apparent to the other tenants. One afternoon at about three o'clock two policemen knocked on the old man's room; and when he opened up they entered and searched it while he tried to decipher the official language of a search warrant. On learning of the intrusion the other tenants were so indignant that they gathered outside the informer's door and shouted threats at him. Even Galton shunned him after that. The old man was well liked in the tenement and no one believed that there was any cause for the police to suspect him of any crime. More than once since the incident the informer planted himself at the foot of the stairs when he heard Galton going out. Beside himself at being ignored, he blocked Galton's way one night and said. "What I do to you, eh? I in' do nothing to you. You in' no better than the rest. I going get you rass! You watch! I going get you rass!" He thereupon got out of Galton's way and went back into his room, full of spleen that Galton had smiled in an expression of contempt, as it seemed to him.

Another night when Galton returned home late from Water Street where he and the watchman had been chatting since early evening he stood face to face with a man dressed in a raincoat and a felt hat who was sitting at the table. Startled by the apparition, he was contemplating what action he ought to take when the man spoke.

"Galton?"

Turning on the light Galton recognised Mr Burrowes, Gemma's father. "How you got in?" he enquired.

"The man downstairs," Gemma's father answered.

"He's got a key?"

"It looks so."

Galton was more stunned by the fact that the informer had in his possession a key to his room than that Gemma's father had come to visit him.

"He's got a key!" he exclaimed in a low voice, as if the significance of the discovery was so stupendous that nothing else mattered.

"All this time he had a key!"

"He isn't the landlord?" asked Mr Burrowes.

"The landlord?" asked Galton mechanically. "No, he isn't the landlord. He's a kind of a friend."

"You mean your friend got a key and you don't even know it?" Mr Burrowes enquired with some surprise.

"Well what's it?" asked Galton.

"I come to see Gemma to find out why she doesn't write," he answered, taking off his hat at the same time.

"She didn't write?" asked Galton.

"No, that's why I came."

Galton went over to the window and opened it almost theatrically.

"She didn't want to live here any more. She left me."

"You blame her?" asked his father-in-law. "Living like this?" and he made a sweeping gesture with his right hand.

"What's wrong with living in here?" shouted Galton. "The place is swarming with people. Some of them've lived here for years. Who the hell is she? You would think she was born in Queenstown! She comes out of a dump like Wismar and lays down conditions for marriage. Why the hell she didn't tell me all that before we were married? She wanted to get that gold ring on her finger so badly she was ready to do anything." Then, in a more conciliatory tone, he continued. "I . . . She couldn't take it any more, and she went off one night . . . took the boat to Surinam—"

"Surinam?" broke in Mr Burrowes. "Surinam? She doesn't know anybody over there. With somebody else?"

"I haven't heard from her since. It's so unusual for her not to write. She liked writing letters," said Galton, ignoring his father-in-law's question. Mr Burrowes got up and came over to Galton.

"She'll write. I know Gemma. She doesn't like hurting people. The trouble with you is you don't know how to deal with women. You have to be more . . . more positive. I might as well tell you: when you were in Linden I put something in your drink to keep you there and make you marry her."

Galton looked at him, astonished at his confession.

"But it didn't work," Gemma's father hastened to add.

"It *did* work," said Galton. "I married her."

"That was a long time after," observed the older man, regretting his moment of weakness.

Galton straightened himself.

"Yes, that was a long time ago," he repeated.

"You're not exactly what I thought you were, you know," said Mr Burrowes. "Going behind my back and talking my name with the Walk-Man."

Galton ignored the remark.

"If you knew him you wouldn't have done it," he pursued. "He caused bad blood between me and his brother. You would think I was a woman the way he was jealous of him. But you, you believe everything he said, just because it suited you. Anyway, what's done's done."

"I never liked you," Galton observed dryly.

"Hm! It's mutual. I can be blunt too, you know. You came into my house pretending you weren't interested in Gemma, and all the time. . . ."

"What?" asked Galton. "I came into your. . . . You think you're talking to some bumpkin in Wismar? I heard about you from the Walk-Man, about the other lodgers in your house. And you yourself just told me about what you put in my drink. With all of that you couldn't even get a man to marry your daughter. I come home to find you sitting in my room, waiting for me like God. It's for *me* to ask you why you enticed me into your house and schemed to make me part of your family. Why? Well, why? What was it that made the others go away and leave her on your hands?"

Mr Burrowes had, until now, taken Galton's mild-mannered behaviour as an indication of an imperturbable docility. Put out by the sudden outburst he could only reply, "Because she didn't want them."

It occurred to Galton that this man's manner and talk had always irritated him, yet he was ready to dismiss him as a fool. But his daughter, whom he had loved, had put gall in his blood and brought him murderous thoughts.

"When she went to Surinam?" asked his father-in-law.

"About three months ago," answered Galton.

"What? And you didn't write and tell me? Three months! And what you doing about it? Did you tell the police?"

"No," came the answer, softly.

"Well, I'm going to tell them," Burrowes said.

He seized his hat from the table and went towards the door. As he was about to open it he hesitated.

"What's her clothes doing here if she's gone away?" asked Mr Burrowes, turning to face Galton.

"That's what I'm wondering myself," replied Galton calmly.

Galton had taken away Gemma's clothes and hidden them after the murder, but a couple of days later, on finding that they were still in their hiding-place, had brought them back and hung them up as she had left them.

In the far corner of the room, behind the table, was her grip.

"I can't understand! How you know she's gone to Surinam?" asked Gemma's father.

"The day before she dis . . . didn't come home she said something about going to Surinam. For all I know she might be next door."

"Why next door?" Mr Burrowes enquired.

"Just a way of talking. I mean she can be anywhere. Look, why not go to the police and get it over with?"

Gemma's father went and sat down again.

"Three months! She never even wrote me she was living in this hole. Why did you leave Peter's Hall? She wrote that it was nice there."

"She wrote that?" asked Galton, springing to life.

"Yes, I've even got the letter here," he declared, fumbling in his pockets. But he was unable to find it.

"You're sure she wrote she liked it? You're sure?" demanded Galton urgently.

"Yes. Why?"

"Nothing," answered Galton.

The feeling of elation, which on more than one occasion when he was under stress had overcome him, now surged through his body.

"She told me she didn't like it there," he informed his father-in-law. "It was she who suggested that we should move."

"She wrote me about the garden and the mosque and how good the people you were living with were to the two of you. I remember it well."

"She wanted her independence," Galton said slowly. "I gave her it . . . because I don't believe in keeping people by you against their will. You can cause them great damage. Great damage! Oh, yes. *Great* damage. People must be free, you see. If they're not free they can't give of their best."

"What're you talking about? You said she left you. Just now you said, they were your own words. Now you say you gave her independence. Tch! You're coming to the station with me?" Mr Burrowes said, seemingly impatient at the prospect of pursuing the conversation.

"What for? You want her found, not me," replied Galton.

His father-in-law left, slamming the door violently behind him.

A moon had come out and cast a pale glow on the table. There, beside the array of tins was yesterday's newspaper, carelessly folded, exposing the front page, on which headlines about a road project to the Brazilian border were printed in very large type. Galton left the room, taking care to lock the door. He went to seek out his friend the watchman. Though it was late January the heavy rains had not come. The damp from the river clung to the piles of wood and the air was heavy with the scent of rot and decay. The lights from the nut sellers' stalls, which fluttered fitfully in the light breeze, would be put out by twelve o'clock, after the last ferry boat had come back. He recalled the fireflies in Linden, cleaving the night like shooting stars. It was thus in Kitty, too, over the wasteland opposite their house, where orchids pilfered the sap of the silk-cotton trees.

EIGHTEEN

Galton's conduct had become so odd over the last three months that the watchman no longer took him to the skipper when he was in port.

"Is what wrong with your friend, man?" the skipper asked the watchman one night. "He come here day-be-fore-yesterday and sit down all day without a word. I mean, if it was in the night I wouldn't mind; but we got a lot of work in the day."

"Why you din' tell he to go home?" asked the watchman.

"I couldn't tell him to go home; he's all right. I give him a bottle of rum and he sit there dozing all morning."

"In the morning?"

"Yes."

"Then he din' go to work," declared the watchman. "They going give he the boot and it going be the ass to play."

Indeed, it was only in the watchman's company that Galton spoke at any length; and if he was asked about Gemma he would fall silent and say nothing for hours afterwards.

More and more he spoke of Selwyn, his brother, recalling especially their youth; and the watchman was not surprised when Galton told him of his decision to take up his brother's offer to live in the bottom flat in Kitty. He had, by this time, had doubts about his friend's sanity and wondered whether, after all, Selwyn's house was the best place for him to live. If his impressions of Selwyn's character were anything to go by he was not capable of keeping the peace between Galton and Nekka.

The watchman helped him to transfer his few possessions from the tenement to David Street.

"You got a nice house hey, man," the watchman said, looking round at the newly decorated flat. "I din' know you had such a posh place. And look at that yard!" he exclaimed, peering out through the lattice-work on the western side.

Although the watchman had spoken the truth the very elegance of the surroundings made his heart sink. The bed in the corner was covered with a blue, tasselled bed-cover. Two wicker armchairs, a writing-table and a rocking-chair made up the rest of the furniture, all new and in good taste.

In the kitchen, at the back, the built-in cupboards over the gas stove and the fittings were all new.

"You brother must spend a lot of money 'pon this. He ask you to pay anything?"

"No. He won't ask for anything."

Galton and the watchman went out into the yard, the latter reflecting that he had misjudged Selwyn.

Across the low, spear-pointed paling staves, they could see a man casting his net in the trench on the other side of the road. A boy stood behind him, holding a basket in his hand. The man pulled the net slowly out of the water and, finding it empty, spread it out on the grass verge, while adjusting its edges here and there. He then took the net up, walked on a bit further, followed by his young companion. His next throw was just as fruitless, but the whole operation was repeated a number of times, until the two were out of sight.

The watchman and Galton stood by the paling. It was late in the morning and groups of secondary-school girls were cycling by on their way from school, little women with books dangling from leather straps tied to their handlebars. Their leisurely way of riding, their exceptionally short skirts, their unconstrained expressions, caught the eye of both men. Within a few minutes their numbers had diminished to the point where only the occasional girl passed, pedalling more hurriedly.

The watchman did not know what to say to his friend.

"Come out of the sun, ne?" he suggested.

Galton followed him inside and sat down.

"It quiet hey, eh? Not like Lombard Street," the watchman observed.

"It quiet, yes."

The two friends talked for about a half an hour and when the watchman got up to go Galton accompanied him to the gate.

On Friday of the following week Galton informed him that he had lost his job. At the workshop it was felt that he was no longer taking an interest in his work.

"You kian' blame them, eh? You would'a do the same in their place," remarked the watchman.

"I going to wait till another job going in Water Street again."

"You going be a watchman again?" asked his friend.

"I don't see why not."

His friend sighed.

"I going keep my ears open. I suppose is the best thing for you to do," said the watchman. "How you did expect to keep you job, not answering people when they talk to you? Is what you trying to do to y'self? Well, I going tell you something straight now: one day they going come for you and tek you away in a ambulance and put you in a strait-jacket. What you going do then? You know what you going do then?"

It was nearly four months before Galton was able to get a job as a watchman in a warehouse in Upper Water Street. He was given a uniform and was required to carry a truncheon. Furthermore, there were occasional checks by the management to ensure that he made his rounds regularly. There was no question of stretching out and going to sleep, or of asking the watchman of the adjoining business to keep an eye on things while he went out on his own business.

The first few days after starting work it was evident that he would have to find another job. He worked at nights only and in the day Selwyn's little boy woke him with his boisterous play. Galton had resolved to have as little as possible to do with his brother and sister-in-law and declined even to mention that the youngster was disturbing his sleep. He gave in his notice at the end of the week, explaining why he could not continue. The manager sympathised with him and added that there was nothing to prevent him applying for the job again once he had found a suitable place to live. Once more Galton was out of work; but as luck would have it a post as sawmill watchman in the stretch of Water Street where his friend worked was to become vacant in a couple of weeks' time. His request to work in the daytime only was rejected, but he agreed to turn on, in the knowledge that he would have to get accustomed to the noise made by his growing nephew while he was sleeping during the day. At least he would be on a night shift every other week.

The day came when he returned to the street in which he used to work before his marriage, where the only sounds were the hooting of ships from the river and the murmur of traffic from Lombard Street.

It was soon after the morning he began working again that he received a letter from his father-in-law, in which he complained that the police were not interested in seeking information about Gemma's whereabouts. People were continually changing their address and if the police pursued enquiries about husbands who had left their wives and wives who had sought refuge with friends the police force would have to be doubled. He asked Galton to write him as soon as he had any news about his daughter and promised, in turn, to do as much for Galton should he hear from her. The letter went on:

Somebody else was enquiring after her. A kind of godfather you might call him. He and Gemma were very close before you got married. He said he is sure Gemma would have come back to Wismar if she had really left you. In his opinion she is in Georgetown and will return to you soon. He thinks that you must move out of that place in Lombard Street. I don't want to rub salt in the wound, Galton, but even her bedroom here is bigger than that place. You only have to hear how Gemma talks to know that she doesn't come from a back yard. I never asked you to do me a favour yet, but I beg you to get out of that place behind a cook-shop. How can a chap with your upbringing ever dream of living there? I know how vexed you must be that I'm harping on the subject, especially as you were so annoyed with me when I brought it up the last time we met. But you know I've got a soft spot for you, Galton. This house is your second home. All you've got to do is say the word and you can come into the shop as a partner. Linden is not a dump. A lot of things are happening here, and there is a new spirit about, since the government nationalised bauxite. I tell you the place has a great future. I've got faith in you, although you lack it in yourself.

I'm no letter-writer, as Gemma was. I prefer to talk. The next time I come to Georgetown I will bring Gemma's "godfather" with me. He's a bit scruffy looking, but as soon as he opens his mouth you'll see he's not of the common run.

Well, Goodbye, boy.

A. H. Burrowes

It was dated weeks before and had only reached Galton by chance. The coughing man had kept it for him and, on learning where Galton was working from the girl who was in the habit of sitting at the passage entrance, brought it round himself.

Since reading the letter Galton became obsessed with the thought of going down to the wharf where he had disposed of his wife. For several days he resisted the temptation, but one night when it was raining and the nut vendors had long since gone home he left his post and made for the wharf, walking briskly. At the junction of Water and Lombard Streets he looked round him at the deserted streets, but did not slacken his pace. When he reached the head of the ramp he looked round him once more and then descended it to the water's edge. He went down on his haunches and dipped his hand in the cold water, closing his eyes as he did so. Were her dresses still hanging on the nails in the room? Of course not! The new tenant must have removed them. It was a rainy night like this, about twenty years ago, when his mother was rocking in her chair and he was waiting for instructions before going to bed. She had asked him to secure a window, through the chinks of which water was seeping. The rain was lashing against the panes, driven by a freak wind.

"The world was so full of sin once, as it is now," she had said to him. "God sent a flood to cover the earth. Imagine the thousands of people that were drowned, swept away from their gambling tables and places of vice. The earth was enveloped in darkness. Your father is a gambler. Galton. He's steeped in sin and shame and

God's mercy is turned away from this house. Kneel down and pray for your father and beg God to spare us and to remember that he was not always like that."

Galton remembered kneeling and praying for his sinful father and secretly begging God that he might at that moment be sheltering from the wind and rain. He imagined him on his bicycle, hatless, making little headway against the wind.

Galton's reflections were interrupted by the sound of a car horn. He could not tell how long he had been squatting by the water. Soaked to the skin, he rose and turned to go, vaguely dissatisfied by his visit to the wharf. When he looked upwards he was suddenly confronted with the figure of a man standing at the head of the ramp. Trying to recall the man's appearance afterwards two points of reference remained in his mind: that his hands were in his pockets and that his feet were turned outwards, in the manner of a man behind a plough.

The words that Galton wanted to utter would not come. He had not been afraid when his father-in-law had questioned him about Gemma, nor when he announced that he was going to the police. Why should this stranger strike terror in his heart, leave him speechless and numb?

When Galton at last was able to uproot himself he mounted the ramp towards the man, who stood his ground. Pretending that he was unconcerned. Galton walked past the motionless figure and in doing so scrutinised his face as best he could in the half light. The stranger was about fifty and of medium height and only his eyes moved as Galton went by.

Instead of going straight down Water Street he made a detour by way of High Street and once back at the sawmill hid behind a pile of wood and waited. It was impossible, in the downpour, to hear approaching footsteps. He thought of putting out the single electric light-bulb, but at once saw the folly of doing so, for thereby he would only attract attention to the sawmill. In High Street there had been no one behind him, so that, in all probability, his fears were groundless. Yet he was barely able to stand upright. His desperation and loss of control were such he kept telling himself that he would do well to go and see his friend further down the road. Then he remembered that he was not on duty.

The rain stopped a short while before Galton was due to be relieved by the day watchman. His clothes were still damp and his shoes, which he had taken off and laid aside, were as soaked as ever. On the arrival of his relief Galton lingered, on the pretext that he was waiting for a friend who would give him a lift home. When the sun came up and the faint hum of cars began to fill the morning he stepped out into the street and made his way towards the bus station, still preoccupied with the idea that the stranger might be somewhere in the vicinity.

Once home Galton changed into dry clothes and went to bed without eating. He reviewed the events of the previous night, coming to the conclusion that he was worrying needlessly. Which passer-by would not stop to see what a man was doing alone at the foot of a ramp in pouring rain? But no sooner had he reassured himself than doubts began to assail him. Why did the man, if he had been a mere passer-by, not go on his way as he, Galton, began to climb the ramp, or speak to him to find out what he had been doing?

"Life is one long hell!" he thought.

It was always like that, except when he was in Selwyn's company as a boy, and enjoyed his protection. The growing away from one another when the latter began courting, the announcement that he would get married soon after he bought the drug-store; and then the news of the marriage itself, when both Selwyn and Nekka must have exposed their love for all to see. And he could imagine the dancing afterwards, the dancing. . . .

For the first time it occurred to Galton that he might be mentally ill. Not, indeed, because he had killed Gemma. He was convinced that any self-respecting man would have done so. Rather, his lack of success at achieving any goal he had set himself and his inability to face up to a situation that had taken him by surprise implanted in his mind the idea that he was progressively losing his grip. The following day, he told himself, he would be in a better position to assess the facts. One gain he had certainly made: he had achieved what he had always longed for, an area that belonged to him alone and from which others could be excluded at will. This thought gave him little comfort when the tenement in Lombard Street came to mind. There, even tenuous relationships now seemed meaningful: the girl in black who took up her position every day at the entrance to the passage was only on nodding terms with him, yet he missed her, it seemed. And those whom he had known quite well, like the informer, now infected his memory in a way he never imagined possible.

Galton fell asleep. And his thoughts pursued him in his sleep. And his dreams protected him from waking. But on waking he could not remember that he had dreamed.

So the months passed, when experiences were scored out with time, like patterns in wet sand.

NINETEEN

It was Christmas Eve night. Galton had just returned from work and was warming up pepperpot which he had kept going for several days. The bell on the gate—attached to it by way of added protection against burglars—rang sharply. Galton ignored it at first, for the watchman always called out before ringing; but in the end the persistent, tinny sound drew him to the door of his flat.

"Everybody's gone out!" Galton shouted.

"You know when they'll be back?" asked the young woman behind the gate.

"No," answered Galton.

"You're Selwyn's brother, aren't you?"

"Yes."

"In a way it's you I want to see," she said.

"Me? About what?" Galton asked, taking a step forward towards the gate.

"Is my radio. Selwyn did promise to ask you to have a look at it for me," said the young woman in a wheedling tone.

"Oh. . . ."

"Don't say no," pleaded the young woman. "Is Christmas and my mother like to listen to the services. Don't say no."

"How far is it?" enquired Galton.

"Just up the road," she hastened to reply.

"All right, but I've got to eat first."

"I can come in?"

"I'll come later if you give me the address," Galton suggested.

"I prefer to wait if you don't mind. Somebody else promise to come and repair it, but din' turn up. I a little anxious, you know," she said.

"All right," Galton gave in reluctantly.

She followed him into the flat.

"It nice here. . . . I does see you passing nearly every day," she said familiarly. Galton did not answer.

"You do you own cooking? I don't like cooking. I don't feel like eating afterwards." She giggled when she said this, not sure whether she was expected to wait in silence or not.

"I related to Nekka, y'know," she informed him. "You musn't tell she I say so. She don't like people to know."

The young woman got up and, without being asked, opened the drawer beneath the built-in cupboard. Taking out the one knife and one of the two forks she laid them on the table beside a plate she found on the draining-board.

"I know you and your brother don't get on. Everybody round here know."

Hardly had she settled in a wicker armchair than she got up again and busied herself with the washing up, which consisted of three plates, one cup and a pan encrusted with a layer of burnt rice.

Galton reckoned that the young woman was offering him an inducement to come and repair her radio. He sat down at table and began breaking his bread, which he dipped in the pepperpot and ate.

She was the very type of woman that Galton could not stand and he was already seeking an excuse to put her off. But he had nowhere to go and a couple of hours spent over a radio would bring him up to bedtime.

While she was washing up her back was turned to Galton, thus affording him an opportunity to scrutinise her from head to foot. She was small in stature with short hair and a rather stout figure. Apparently unable to be still for a moment she gave the impression of being wound up.

"I had a bicycle up to yesterday," she said, turning round to address Galton, "but somebody steal it; from our own yard. I don't know."

Then Galton's words came, despite himself: "You could've borrowed mine, if I had one."

He looked up at her apologetically, and she stopped wiping the plates momentarily and smiled without answering. She was thinking that it was odd that man of his looks had never been seen with a woman. After all he was not a cripple. Since his remark about the bicycle she had come to feel shy in his presence. He, in turn, took care to make less noise while eating.

When he had finished his dinner he got up and placed the plate with the knife and fork in the sink.

"Leave that. I'll do it," he said.

"No, I might as well do it with the others," she protested.

She now seemed to Galton less brash, more intelligent.

They left the house together and Galton took care to open the gate for her. At her gate he went ahead and opened it as well. Her mother came out to introduce herself and it was only after the first cautious, embarrassed remarks that he noticed a slight figure in a corner of the gallery, its head adorned with a green peak to keep the lamplight from his eyes. Galton nodded, but only received a barely recognisable acknowledgement. The head turned away and resumed its attitude of intense concentration over the large, open volume on the writing table.

"He come for the radio, Father," said Nekka's cousin, but her father paid her no attention at all.

The young lady's mother remained, hovering over them as if afraid that her departure might be interpreted as an unsociable act. Every time Galton caught her eye she smiled radiantly and when her daughter said she was going inside to fetch the radio she volunteered to go instead and went off, cooing like a pigeon on a September morning.

"My name's Mildred," Nekka's cousin said, inviting him to follow her into the dining-room.

On returning. Mildred's mother placed the ancient set on the dining-table, then waited to see what he would do. Galton took out a screwdriver from his trouser pocket and set about opening the panel which enclosed the array of tubes and wires.

"Why not get some drink for Mr Flood?" Mildred's mother said to her daughter, who was anxious to know whether the damage could be repaired that very night. Mildred did as she was told and before long a tray with black cake and fly was set before him.

"Why not take it now?" asked Mildred's mother.

Galton looked at Mildred, put down his screwdriver and reached for the glass of foaming Christmas drink, which must have been fermenting in a cupboard over the last few weeks.

"Mother, you embarrassing Mr Flood," Mildred said, at the end of her patience.

"All right," her mother answered, with an expression of such indulgence that Galton censured Mildred with a brief glance.

Galton and Mildred were left alone. The house reminded him of those old homes he and Selwyn were made to visit when they were young children, with rocking-chairs and walls hung with old photographs.

Mildred took away the tray when he had finished, then came back to watch him repair the radio. The blare of music brought her mother out from the bedroom.

"It working!" she exclaimed.

"You satisfied now?" came a voice all the way from the gallery.

"How much it is?" asked Mildred, rising from her seat.

"Oh, it's a Christmas present," said Galton.

"Thank you," Mildred's mother fairly shouted.

"Its only a box with wires!" the voice from the gallery chided.

Mildred saw Galton to the door, accompanied by music from the newly repaired radio. As soon as he had completed work on the set he decided to ask Mildred if he could see her again; he would wait till they were alone on the porch. But on the porch his courage failed him.

"Don't forget not to tell Nekka I say I'm her cousin," said Mildred. "Since she married your brother she don't own up to us."

"I won't say anything," answered Galton, prolonging the moment of his going. At the gate he thought he heard her say "Goodbye" again, but did not turn round.

Galton, unable to restrain his desire to see Mildred once more, went boldly to her house the next night. She welcomed him as if she were expecting to see him. Her father was in the same corner, but her mother did not come out.

Mildred was not as zestful as the night before and at Galton's attempts to make conversation she gave short, almost curt answers. Now there was no doubt in his mind that her manner the night before had been inspired by the need to have her radio set repaired before Christmas Day. After all, she had not invited him back.

It was only when Galton got up to go, much earlier than he had intended, that her disappointment provided proof of her desire to continue seeing him.

"Did I offend you?" he asked her.

"No. I did think I offended you."

"You? No."

Smiling at him, she gradually came out of her shell, and their conversation was accompanied by the sound of carols from inside. That night she went with him once more to the porch and this time he turned round some distance from the house.

Every night when he was on day duty Galton went to Mildred's house where he remained in a huddle with her at the dining-table. Her mother somehow contrived to be inside on his arrival and he only saw her once in a while, usually on her way from the bedroom to the kitchen and back from the kitchen to the bedroom.

One night Mildred's father was not in his accustomed place. She declared that he was ill and confined to bed with a thermometer and his books.

"Let's go and sit in the gallery, ne," suggested Mildred. They got up to go to the front of the house into the part of the gallery where they would be alone.

For a long time they sat in silence and when Galton pulled her from her chair she asked feebly, "Suppose Ma come?" Galton embraced her and she muttered, "No, no, Galton."

"Let's go to my flat, then," he said, hopefully.

"Only if you promise not to interfere with me."

Mildred opened and closed the door as quietly as possible and they hurried up the road, pursued by shadows and the chirping of crickets.

Galton made her sit down on his bed; when he put his hand on her thigh she pressed her lips against his more firmly than ever.

On re-emerging into the night they saw that the lights in all the houses in the street were off.

"They'll be vexed at home?" Galton asked.

"Naw! Father won't know I've been out and Mother won't tell him," said Mildred.

She clung to him on the way to her house and extracted from him a promise to come and see her the next night. As he made his way back down the road she stood watching through the glass; then, losing sight of him among the shadows, leaned her forehead against the pane.

TWENTY

It was a Sunday afternoon that Jessie came to see Selwyn. Thelma was with her. She had grown into a young woman of extraordinary ugliness, old for her fourteen-odd years and her face covered in pimples. Jessie looked more distinguished than ever with her smooth, broad brow and greying hair. She enquired after Galton, who was at work, and informed Nekka and Selwyn that Winston had been declared bankrupt. Their house at Peter's Hall had been sold to pay their debts and they were living in a small house on the public road. She had to interrupt her account as she spoke of the house, so overwrought she was.

"Winston wants to see Galton," she said to Selwyn.

"He does hardly talk to us," Nekka said.

"I'll tell him," Selwyn assured her.

"Where's he live?" enquired Jessie.

"Downstairs . . . you didn't know?" asked Selwyn.

"No. We heard he was somewhere in Lombard Street," said Jessie.

"Selwyn built on a flat for him and furnish it better than ours," said Nekka bitterly. "And he's hardly say 'good morning' or 'good night.' He's only talk to Sonnie."

"Who's Sonnie?"

"Our boy," said Selwyn.

"He talks already?" asked Jessie, with surprise.

"He's over three." Nekka informed her. "Sonnie?" she called out, and a little boy came out of the back, where he had been hiding from the strangers. Jessie put out both arms to the child, who made his way as slowly as possible towards her.

"Say hello to Auntie Jessie," ordered Nekka to the frightened child.

"Take your thumb out of your mouth!" his father said imperiously.

Thelma looked on, aloof. Bored by the behaviour of the grown-ups she peered at them through her glasses, not attempting to conceal her contempt. Her mother had long ago learned not to say, "Kiss Aunt So-and-So, Thelma!" for Thelma would refuse bluntly and embarrass everybody.

"Go and say hello to Thelma," Selwyn urged his little boy, thinking that the youngster might be more willing to approach a younger person. "Go on!" Then turning proudly to Jessie, Selwyn announced, "He was talking before he was a year old."

"Is true!" Nekka confirmed, pushing the little boy towards Thelma. He refused to go in Thelma's direction, however, intimidated possibly by her hostile glare or the unusual geography of her face.

"Go on!" insisted Nekka. The boy burst into tears, turned round and took refuge in his mother's arms.

"What kind of foolishness is this at all?" Selwyn said severely, ashamed at his son's behaviour. But his mother kissed her son by way of consolation. Inwardly, she was angry with Thelma for failing to encourage her first-born.

Selwyn, on the point of launching into a description of how they designed and built the flat under the house, thought better of it when he remembered that Winston and Jessie had just lost their home. In fact, all the things he wanted to talk about would have constituted an indiscretion, in the circumstances.

"What about Winston's partner?" asked Selwyn.

"He and his partner broke up long before this business," Jessie replied, "because he said Winston was too extravagant. Winston couldn't get anybody to sell him beef on credit when they heard things were going badly. And the other day at Golden Grove the people he used to buy pigs from hid in their houses when they heard he had come. At least two of them made a lot of money through Winston. He never once let a pig-keeper down. That's why they went to hide: they were afraid to face him. One man had a few scraggly pigs when Galton started buying from him. None of the other butchers would buy his animals. Now he's one of the biggest pig-keepers in the village; but when Winston went and knocked on his door his little daughter opened and said her father had gone to Mahaicony. All of these people did drink his rum and laugh with him when he had money or could do them a favour."

Jessie delved into her handbag hurriedly and took out a handkerchief with which she daubed her eyes. Selwyn, confused, felt powerless to console her. His drugstore was doing excellent business, and every word that defined the disaster that had befallen his acquaintance brought him satisfaction, despite himself.

"If I can help," he said tentatively.

Jessie looked away and Selwyn got up, went inside and came back soon afterwards with a wad of notes. He took her right hand in his and closed her fingers over the bundle. She burst into tears in front of Nekka, Selwyn, her daughter and the bewildered child, who, himself, had been bawling a few minutes earlier.

"She lost something. Ma?" asked Sonnie.

Nekka took him to the back of the house.

Selwyn drove Jessie and Thelma home, past the Sunday afternoon strollers in their Sunday best and the black-pudding stalls with their bottle-lamps, preparing for the return of the strollers after dark.

Winston was out and so he drove back home to discuss his plight with Nekka.

As he went up the stairs he heard her singing. Their baby daughter was on her lap drinking milk from a bottle, while Sonnie was standing beside her, his thumb in his mouth and his eyes half-closed.

"You see him?" asked Nekka.

"No, he was out."

"Don't forget to tell Galton what she say. You know him; if he don't get the message he's swear you do it on purpose and he might even. . . .

"Be quiet!" Selwyn said.

Sonnie opened his eyes wide and then closed them completely when he saw that his parents were not going to have an argument.

"You better put him to bed," Nekka advised, nodding at her son.

Selwyn took his young son by the hand. "Ma cleaned your teeth?" he asked him.

"Yes."

Selwyn undressed him, put him to bed and kissed him on his cheek.

"Sleep well, son. Ma's coming in a minute to tell you a story," he told him, knowing that his son was likely to be asleep by the time his mother came.

Selwyn went and sat down by the window. In his mind he recapitulated the accounts of the last week and wondered if he, too, might not, one day, suffer Winston's fate. No one had been as confident as Winston; no one looked more secure than he. His table had always been provided with large tureens of soup, dishes laden with meat and an assortment of ripe fruit. His friends and his friends' friends were always welcome in his home and at his table and, indeed, often took advantage of his hospitality, so that, at times, his house resembled a club or the forecourt of a cinema.

"What you thinking 'bout?" asked Nekka, who had come to join him after putting the girl to bed. "You know you kian' do nothing. You kian' pay his debts, after all. That money you give him mek a big hole in you pocket, but in' go'n mek much difference to them."

Selwyn dismissed her words with a wave of his hand. Nobody could reduce a situation to its material elements more readily than Nekka, he thought. What was preoccupying him was not his sympathy for Winston, but rather his lack of concern. He despised himself for wanting to go to the pictures or to play bridge with his friends an hour after Jessie had been telling him of the misfortunes that had befallen her household.

"Why you don't find something to do, ne?" he asked Nekka, speaking harshly.

"What wrong with you? I been working all day. Just 'cause you waste you money on people you in' see for months you don't got to tek it out on me!"

She got up, snatched a newspaper lying on the rocking-chair and went into the spare bedroom, which had not been used since Galton's first stay with them. Lying full-length on the bed she raised the paper above her head and began reading.

Selwyn sat by the window until he saw Galton coming down the road. Lately, his step was more purposeful. But he seemed more evasive than ever. To make certain that his brother did not lock himself in before he could talk to him, Selwyn cut him off at the gate.

"Jessie's been."

"And?" asked Galton, without encouragement.

"Winston's gone bankrupt."

Galton made an "O" with his lips, but uttered no sound. Then, after a moment's reflection, he said brutally, "And what you want me to do?"

"Nothing," Selwyn replied. "She said he wanted to see you; I don't know why."

Galton stood beside his brother as if turning over something in his mind, then said, "I don't have the time," and went past him. But Selwyn retained him by seizing his arm.

"Come up and have a shot, ne?"

"Y'know I don't drink," Galton said sharply.

"You don't. . . ."

Selwyn thought it best to humour him.

"What kind of uncle you are to these two children, eh?" he asked. "For all the time you've been back you haven't come up once. Not once! Nekka says you treat her like a leper. How can you live in the same house and ignore somebody the way you ignore her? I know she isn't bright. Christ! But there're other things in the world besides intellect."

Selwyn might have been speaking to the door post. His brother was looking right through him at something far beyond him; or perhaps deep into him. The head, the trunk, the legs were Galton's, but some profound change had taken place. Selwyn believed that Galton was anxious to avoid contact with him lest he discover the nature of the metamorphosis.

Galton glanced upwards and saw Nekka staring down at them through the open window. He abruptly broke off and went inside. Selwyn looked up in turn and saw his wife.

"Skunt!" he muttered to himself. Then aloud to her, "I'm just going down the road for some cigarettes."

He started off in the direction of the railway crossing. The appearance of the parallel steel lines, gleaming under the street lamps, seemed to belie the fact that the railway was closed down. Those trains day in day out, bursting with people, dividing the sweltering days with their hissing and hooting, crawling the fifty-odd miles from Georgetown to Rossignol along the flat Guyana coastlands like rattling caterpillars, were gone for ever.

Selwyn gave a rail a gentle kick, in the absurd expectation that it would move.

When he got back home there was no light, either downstairs or upstairs. Nekka must have gone to bed in disgust.

TWENTY-ONE

Mildred had gone to Bartica to see her relations and Galton took advantage of her absence to look up the watchman.

"Eh, eh, stranger! I thought I did do you something. Who would think we working in the same street?" burst out the watchman, delighted at seeing Galton for the first time in months.

"I've been busy," Galton told him.

"Don't give me that! I bet you courting!"

To the watchman's surprise he saw that his remark, made in jest, had struck home.

"Is true, then?" he enquired of Galton, who was reluctant to admit that he was courting again.

"It's a girl living in David Street. I never thought. . . ."

Galton, excessively cautious by temperament, did not want to tempt fate by admitting that Mildred was the perfect companion.

"She's a good woman," he said finally.

"I can see that by you shoes," joked the watchman.

"My shoes?"

"Yes, man. You cleaning them!" exclaimed the watchman, trying to suppress a laugh and pointing at Galton's feet.

"Good giaff go with good rum," said the watchman, who disappeared behind the mountain of wood.

Galton, just off duty, was not keen on engaging in a drinking bout with his friend, who had all night before him. Just as he reappeared, a bottle of rum in his hand and tripping With pleasure at his friend's unexpected visit, a lorry drew up in front of the sawmill, laden with wallaba.

"Oh, rass! Just my luck," he said to Galton; and then, addressing the chauffeur, who was in the act of jumping down from his lorry, he asked sarcastically: "Why you din' come at midnight? We would 'a really mek it a party."

The chauffeur and the three men who had been sitting on the pile of lumber, spent the better part of an hour unloading and stacking the beams.

"What they for? Lamp-posts?" asked the watchman, while signing the delivery note.

"It look so," replied one of the men.

"Well, they kian' cut that for a few days yet," mocked the watchman.

"You talking as if you got shares in the business, man. I don't care if they cut it next year," remarked the chauffeur. By the way of a parting shot, he added: "Don't kill yourself with work tonight. I know a watchman dead from overwork last year. He had a big funeral. Guyanese got a funny sense of humour."

The lorry moved off, its engine roaring.

"I'm only having one," Galton told his friend. "I was on my way home to sleep."

"I forget, I forget," declared his friend. "It don't matter. One, two, six: what's the difference?"

They drank the rum straight from the bottle, smacking their lips to cool the fire in their mouths.

"You remember that chap I used to live at? Just after I got married," asked Galton.

"Up at Peter's Hall?"

"Yes," Galton confirmed. "He's bankrupt."

"Bankrupt? You mean he business gone?"

"Yes. He can't pay his debts. So they sell the business to pay off the people he owes."

"That bad. People don't go bankrupt like in the old days. How he tekking it?"

"I dunno," replied Galton. "His wife was telling my brother."

"Anyway," observed the watchman. "That's one thing we kian' get. That's rich man disease."

He handed Galton the bottle and as the latter was about to protest, said, "One for the road, for the road!"

They both took a quick swig and once more smacked their lips.

"You looking good, y'know," said the older man. He wanted to add, "Since you lashing regular." But he thought that perhaps Galton was not ready for that kind of talk.

"What about the children mekking noise when you sleeping?" the watchman prodded.

"Oh, I'm not really accustomed to it, but it doesn't bother me much."

"And you sister-in-law?"

"She and I hardly see each other."

Galton had evaded the question. By now he was able to judge just what sort of wife Nekka was. Much to his astonishment she and Selwyn did not quarrel as much as he imagined. Furthermore, she possessed qualities he never attributed to her. She was a good mother and an attentive wife.

The watchman sensed Galton's disappointment that Nekka was not the wretch he had imagined her to be. He changed the subject in an attempt to evoke a response in his friend that might lead to a decent conversation. But his questions were only answered in monosyllables. That was Galton! he thought. One word, one look and he withdrew into his shell. He had learned that it was fatal to insist.

"I'll come and see you tomorrow," Galton said. "Mildred's in Bartica."

"All right. I going get the wife to mek cook-up rice and shrimps and we going dove a cuttie or something."

"See you," Galton said and left his friend.

"See you, then."

The watchman saw his friend up the road and imagined him getting into a taxi with four or five other people.

"At least he goin' have company on the way home," he thought.

Galton came the next night as he had promised. He laughed and joked with his friend, congratulated him on the cook-up rice and stayed to drink not only the cuttie of rum, but went to the liquor restaurant where he bought a half-bottle to drown the cook-up rice, as he put it.

"I'm kindly disposed to the whole world tonight," said Galton with a flourish. "No hate! No rancour! You can't blame the dog if you fall off your cycle, eh? No. Tonight is the night of forgiveness and compassion. I. . . . You listening?"

"Yes," the watchman hastened to add.

"I got a lot of love in me," Galton continued. "It's true!" he protested, although the watchman had said nothing to contradict him. "I got more love than all of you put together—in this street, in Lombard Street, in all the streets from here to Sherrif Street. . . . You sleeping, my friend?"

Galton put his hand on his friend's head.

"No. I only close me eyes to stop me head from spinning."

"Sleep, my friend, sleep. I feel like shouting. But they'd only arrest me. If a man from Lombard Street were to shout. . . . Doesn't matter. Tonight I could drink a bottle of rum big enough to fill the Demerara River. Sleep, my friend, and when you've had your fill you must talk to me as in the old days. I miss that alleyway. . . . My eyes are failing, my hair is greying; only my morality is intact. What do you all know of love, eh?"

Every night Galton came to drink with his friend, but on the eighth day when his tour of night duty came round, he stayed home to visit Mildred, who had just returned. People in the street said she had put a noose round his neck, in the manner of the iguana hunters.

That night they waited until her parents had gone to bed and made love on the floor, for, after that first night, she would not go home to him again, deeming it to be immoral to visit a man in his home. She preferred to make love on the floorboards of her own house rather than in the bed of his flat.

In the months that followed Galton was so happy he had taken to sitting on the porch and conversing with Selwyn through the window. The latter was unable to tempt him in or to effect a reconciliation between him and Nekka, but she at least saw in his behaviour the signs of a more cordial relationship in the future.

The large family next door had moved out and an East Indian family from La Bonne Intention had moved in. Selwyn was surprised at the speed with which Galton had struck up an acquaintanceship with the father of the family.

"Is what your cousin done to my brother?" Selwyn asked his wife jokingly. "He's behaving as if he's normal."

Indeed, Galton was so happy that when the informer came to look him up he was not in the least suspicious about it.

"I come to sympathise. Somebody tell me you wife left you. I got a conscience too, y'know. Is me did tell you 'bout the visitor; and you know, meddling in everything and knowing everything that happening in the tenement getting to be a burden."

Somehow Galton had forgotten that it was the informer who had alerted him to Gemma's visits. A shadow came over his face and he shuddered at the realisation that this man was capable of stirring all the old hatreds and anxieties with a single remark. On seeing him he was ready to talk over old times, the tenement dwellers like the coughing man and the fat girl: and here he was, trembling lest the informer was in possession of knowledge that could damn him and ruin his new-found happiness. If it were so he would not hesitate to use it in some way.

"You know, though we had all them quarrels," said the informer, "I kian' forget how you give me coffee and all them things. Nowadays people don't give, y'know. They kian' afford to. Eh, eh! In these hard gauva-days even wild bush cost money. And me with a thirst for good living. I tell you, it does lef' me throat dry. I like suede shoes and . . . but you not interested, I can see. I like me person. My person. You feel me hands. Go on! Feel how soft they is."

"I take your word for it," Galton said, praying that his visitor would come to the point.

"You're so trusting, mister. That's why everybody like you. Is funny, I not like that. When I meet a trusting man I does get vexed and work meself up in a state. Not with you, though. I know you. No, I talking 'bout strangers. But is funny, everybody like you, but you not a happy person. Go on, admit it. You does get depressed and thing, in't it? Go on, admit it. Not me, people don't like me. But depression in't my way. Tears and tearing out my hair and chest pounding, I don't understand it. My mother like that too. You meet my mother, didn't you? Oh, yes, at my place. You mek a impression. But she never mention you name since. She's like that. Like me. We don't got a talent for friendship. Wha' for do? We kian' help it. . . . Funny, talking to you here in your place is different. It not so tense as in the tenement. Here I feel . . . kinda clean. See what money can do! If I did feel like peeing in this road I'd rather let me bladder burst first. Yes!"

He stopped for a while, but seeing that Galton would say nothing, continued.

"How you father-in-law?"

"I don't know," answered Galton. "I haven't heard from him."

"Oh, I did only let him into you room 'cause you all is family. Don't think I wanted to be officious. After all, you don't got nothing to hide. Not like me. For country people they talk good, you father-in-law and you wife that lef' you. Is people you would be proud to walk round with. 'This is my family,' you would say and by the cut of they jib and their grammar people know what they like and what *you* like. 'Cause like attract like. By the way, is who you wife run off wit'?"

Galton looked at him darkly.

"No offence. Don't look at me like that. If a friend kian' ask a personal question is what friendship for? Mind you, I ask it out of concern: you see they got some suspicious people who say she in' run off wit' nobody. Somebody in the tenement had a dream that she come to them crying and begging for help."

"Who had the dream?" Galton demanded.

"The coughing man. You can go and ask him. . . . Come to think of it, it mek sense. In this country somebody would see you wife sooner or later and would come and tell you, if she did really run off wit' a man. After all, if you fart in Skeldon everybody know in the north-west. But this dream. . . . I dunno. A nice girl like that, so well-mannered. When I hear it I get a shiver down to the bone and when I going to sleep I stuff cloth under the door, 'cause I know she din' like me. . . . Anyway, I thought I'd come and tell you what people thinking and saying. Yes, is a difference, y'know. If they was just thinking . . . but saying and all! Anyway, I gone."

He got up and made for the door, keeping an eye on Galton at the same time. Then, wheeling round as if suddenly recognising a danger, he said, "You think I's a fool! I did want to test you, rouse you like, get you blood up. You won't got the guts to touch you wife. After all you and she live above me. You never beat she once. When everybody else was quarrelling and fighting all you was always calm. I in't say *happy,* mind you. But calm. I mean they in' got nobody more calm than the dead. But they in' happy. . . . What's you game, eh? You wouldn't let me stand here insulting you if something wasn't wrong. When I enter this first-class downstairs flat I say to meself, 'I kian' insult he here!' You don't insult a man in these surroundings. Lattice-work, a yard with fruit trees, crabwood cupboard, man . . . I know 'bout quiet people. All that pent-up energy must come out some time. Anyway, this time I gone. And seeing as how you din' offer me nothing I think I doing the right thing to be going."

Galton, left alone, wondered whether he ought to have threatened the informer. Recalling how easily the latter was frightened he pondered the idea of visiting him in the tenement, but decided that it was too risky. Should he go and see the coughing man to find out about the dream? That would be playing into the informer's hands, Galton concluded, rejecting that idea as well.

Mildred noticed that he was not himself.

"What's wrong?" she enquired.

"A chap came to see me. It's nothing."

"Yes, it's something," she objected.

"I must tell you," he said.

"Go on."

"I was in love with my wife."

"I knew that, Galton."

"But something happened. Something bad happened."

"I know. She did leave you. Why talk about it?"

"I don't go to church any more. I see you passing with your mother and father on Sundays," he said, avoiding the confession he had intended making.

"That's all?" she asked, smiling with relief.

"That's all. . . . When you saw me, the first time you saw me, did I look like a criminal?"

"You?" she asked, surprised and anxious. "Ma say if she had a rabbit to kill it'd be no use asking you. Pa can do it without even looking up from his books. But why you want to know? Somebody say something to you?"

"No, it's nothing."

"You miss her?" Mildred asked.

"I don't think so."

"Oh."

She was hurt that Galton's answer had not been more definite. He never spoke of his wife and Mildred wondered why.

"I think you still in love with her."

"No!" Galton answered, not realising how much satisfaction Mildred drew from the vehemence in his voice.

From then on Galton never missed an opportunity to be with Mildred on his nights off. Until then he had skipped Saturdays and Sundays, out of propriety, he told his mistress's mother. But once he was assured of Mildred's and her mother's approval he treated weekends as he had done the weekdays. And the informer's visit was soon forgotten, like those brief storms that break into a succession of cloudless days.

The day the government party won the elections Mildred's father, an ardent supporter of the ruling party, invited Galton on a trip up the east coast in a hired car. It was the first overt gesture of acceptance made to him by this enigmatic man, whose voracious appetite for books excluded everyone from the mysterious circle that seemed to surround him.

Mildred's father enquired of the driver where they could stop off and have something in a "decent place." He recommended a new establishment at Bachelor's Adventure, where the ladies stepped demurely from the hired car. Mildred's mother, unaccustomed to the luxury of an outing, was wearing a frightened expression and Mildred herself looked for all the world like a Sunday school teacher who had strayed too far from her Sunday school. Galton sipped fruit juice in silence, while Mildred's father tried to fend off the owner's attempts at conversation.

Mildred openly demonstrated her affection for Galton, taking his hand in hers and nestling up to him on the bench where they sat. She had taken her father's invitation to Galton as the seal of approval of their liaison.

When they stepped outside they found the chauffeur asleep. Night had drawn its blanket across the sky and the surrounding landscape, dotted here and there with trees, was bleak. Bats were darting about the bushes in search of insects, their high-pitched squeaking hardly audible in the oppressive stillness.

Along the road groups of government supporters waved to the car as it went by and shouted slogans. On one shop sign with "X-M Rum" painted boldly in red had been draped a slogan of which only the word "Vote" was now visible.

In the back of the car Mildred was leaning heavily on Galton, while her mother kept her eyes glued to the swiftly moving landscape. Mildred's father, who was sitting beside the chauffeur, was looking straight ahead.

"Nice houses, eh?" he remarked.

"Yes," agreed his wife.

"Indians living in most of them," he pursued.

The chauffeur, himself an Indian, drove serenely on.

"A new road's coming straight through there," Mildred's father said, pointing to the grounds in the middle of which a mansion stood. "D'Aguiar lives there."

"They'll pull it down?" his wife enquired.

"I suppose so," came the answer.

She looked back at the house through the rear window.

When the car drew up in front of his own house Mildred's father paid the chauffeur and followed the others up the stairs, pleased that the outing had been enjoyed by everyone.

"When's the next election?" he asked, speaking to no one in particular.

"In five years, I think," said Galton.

"Well, the next time we'll go right up to Mahaica and watch the sun come up. That's something, I hear."

He settled down in his corner and waited for his wife to bring his mug of cocoa.

The next time Galton went to Mildred's house her mother answered the door. She came out on the landing to meet him instead of letting him in as Mildred did. Through the window he could see that her father was not in his accustomed place, at the writing desk.

"My husband ask me to tell you not to come back here," she announced, avoiding his gaze.

Galton looked at her in disbelief.

"Why?" he could barely articulate.

"He say there's no future in you visiting Mildred, being married and all."

Her voice seemed strained to Galton.

"All right, goodnight," he said, turning to go. "C— can I see Mildred? For a short while?" he stammered.

"*I* don't mind," she whispered. "But he set his mind against it. You better go now. He boiling up inside the bedroom and I going have to tell him just what you say."

Galton went down the stairs.

At home he stood in the middle of the front room, staring through the lattice-work. It was all so sudden, like being struck on the head with a stick from behind. That house with its shaky bannisters was closed to him for good. They must have been aware of the intimacy between Mildred and himself. Why condone it, knowing that he was married and, months later, put a stop to it *because* he was married? The watchman had reproached him for not being a fighter. How could he fight a man in his own house? If there had been a scene everyone in the street would have known why he could no longer go back to the house.

It was one morning while he was on his way home on foot that the solution to the riddle of his banishment from Mildred's house came to Galton. He stood on the pavement at the crossroads, staring straight ahead without seeing the carts, the bicycles, the cars or the passers-by. The night when he was reviewing every clue, every possibility, how could he have neglected the most obvious, the *nearest* clue? There he was standing in his flat under the house where the rat was sniffing about, looking into corners, testing openings with its whiskers, plotting a night's work; and he had failed to detect the vermin's presence. Nekka! It was Nekka who must have told Mildred's family something about his past. Of course! Why then was he prevented from seeing Mildred? He knew of people whose relations were brought to an end by one word from some envious onlooker. Yes! There was Nancy, who, soon after her engagement, broke it off because she was told that her young man's family had a history of leprosy. He remembered the business well, because Selwyn had been taken to the engagement party by his mother and when he came back he described the food they had eaten so vividly that he, Galton, went into a corner and sulked for hours. It was only a few days later that they heard the news that the betrothal had been brought to an end.

Nekka! She could not stand Mildred and she hated him. What was more natural than that she should seek to separate them? That night he had caught her looking at him and Selwyn from the window. He recalled how a shiver had run through his body on perceiving that figure at the window; how, when he looked up, she stood her ground brazenly, defying him to hold her gaze. In the half light he could define the arrogant curl of her upper lip, the heavy scent of perfume that surrounded her. Oh, yes! Among the young coconut there always lurked a centipede;

among the orchids a venomous labaria, unseen, but seeing all around it with its consuming stare.

Galton was attracting the attention of passers-by, who turned round to stare at him.

"You all right, friend?" asked a young man who had stopped beside him.

"Eh?" asked Galton.

"You all right?" came the question once more.

"Why?"

The young man made a gesture with his hands.

"I just thought something was wrong," he answered.

"I just made a discovery," Galton said softly, and a smile appeared on his face.

The young man edged away from him and, seeing that Galton wanted to pursue the conversation, walked away quickly.

"I thought you wanted to talk," Galton muttered to himself. "I thought you wanted to talk."

Galton walked on, very slowly, as if the weight of his reflections was keeping him back.

In the broad daylight he was suddenly assailed by a vision of the alleyway behind the tenement in Lombard Street. He turned back and retraced his steps. On reaching Lombard Street he had some difficulty in finding it, for he had to take the side street that connected Lombard Street with High Street and watch carefully for every unlikely opening. Finally, beside an incredibly dingy cake-shop he saw the gutter with earth rising on each side. Without hesitating he turned into the passage. Pieces of wood and all kinds of rubbish were strewn pell-mell on both sides of the gutter. When he got to the section he used to watch from the tenement he looked up at the window where he and Gemma had lived. A mattress and bedding were hanging out of it to catch the brief rays of sunlight before the sun reached the high building on the other side. Two women were talking behind the corrugated-iron fence and he could hear what they were saying distinctly.

"You in' look so good, y'know."

"Na, chile; I got me things."

"Ah! That's life, eh."

They had nothing more to say to each other. Galton spat involuntarily. He looked up again at the window, stared at it for several minutes before he heard someone coming down the alleyway from the opposite direction to the one from which he had come. Galton walked on and passed an old man who looked at him suspiciously.

"It was the worst mistake of my life," he thought, "moving from the tenement. Now everything is at an end, all the pain, all the pain. There must be no suffering, no pain. Suffering was in childhood, that unending strand of deprivation." The violence that had welled up in him on discovering what Nekka had done was now gone, and now he was sorry for her. All those closest to him had been cut off from him, their relations severed by some incomprehensible act of fate; his father had died suddenly; his brother had got married and Mildred had decided in one night to fall out of love with him. Since those were the terms of living there was to be no emotion. It must be ripped out and put away in some high, inaccessible tree, like the intestines of soldiers wrenched away by the vultures in Li Po's poem. Just the sight of the alleyway and the window of his erstwhile lodging place had allowed him to put things in perspective. All these words, these reflections, were pointless. They were the haze through which one looked at life. . . . Tomorrow he must go and see Winston in Peter's Hall to show him that there was no resentment.

Galton walked briskly to avoid the full force of the sun, which had by now risen high over the horizon. At home he took a long shower, made breakfast and then lay down to sleep. He heard Nekka come down into the yard and go upstairs again. Sleep must have come soon afterwards, for he remembered nothing more.

The next day Mildred told Selwyn what had really caused the break between herself and Galton.

It was precisely Galton's intimacy with her which threw her father into confusion. Though Galton would have found it hard to believe, the older man did not realise how close the two young people were before he saw them huddled against each other in the eating place and in the car. The countless occasions when she yielded to him had passed without arousing his suspicions; and though her mother knew what was going on she hid it from her husband, for she liked Galton.

On their return from Bachelor's Adventure there had been a terrible row. Mildred's father accused his wife of encouraging Galton to take liberties with their daughter.

"You mean all this time you think they was holding hands in the dining-room?" she asked him.

"Not even that!" he answered indignantly. "I'm not running a brothel."

Her mother took fright at the turn of the conversation and did not have it out with him.

Mildred finally spoke.

"I love him."

This simple statement put her father into such a fury he stamped on the floor and informed his daughter that he would not be crossed in his own house. The matter was settled: much as she brought in some money from her part-time job she depended upon him for the clothes on her back, and he reserved the right to choose who was suitable for her. Mildred bowed to superior reason.

The only question left to decide was who should inform Galton of the decision. Mildred refused. Her father thought it was not necessary for him to be cast in a villainous role, as he and Galton had always got on well. There was no doubt that the obvious person to tell the young man was his wife. Mildred's mother asserted that it was she who had got on well with Galton, and as far as she could judge, her husband and Galton had no relationship whatsoever. Nevertheless, she obeyed.

After Galton had been sent away from the house Mildred's father sat down and wrote him a letter explaining his decision, but tore it up after his wife and daughter had read it. There was no reason to feel guilty about his decision or the way he acted. When, later, Mildred's mother asked him what it was he had objected to in Galton, that he was married or that he had become intimate with Mildred, he answered, "To tell the truth I don't know. If he knew how to behave I wouldn't have objected just because he was married."

"I wonder what you learn in all them books?" she asked.

"I don't expect you to understand," he countered, feeling sorry for his ignorant wife.

Selwyn informed Galton of his conversation with Mildred. From then on Galton could no longer go past her house. The sight of her father's head adorned with its green peak, its ears covered by two hands in an attitude of concentration, stirred in him an indescribable longing.

TWENTY-TWO

The following Monday evening Galton was free. Having washed and shaved after a day in bed he walked to Stabroek and there took a hired car to Peter's Hall. He had declined Selwyn's offer to drive him there.

Galton knew that Winston's rented house was small, but he had not been prepared for such a tiny dwelling, separated from the grass verge by a gutter half-choked with grass. He spotted Thelma, who promptly disappeared from the window, no doubt to alert her parents to his arrival. Before he could even knock a voice boomed at him through the open window.

"Push, man! It's open."

Winston was sprawled out on a Berbice chair, one leg raised on the extendible bar. Beaming up at Galton he offered him a hand.

"Man! Is where they dig people like you up from?" asked Winston, as light-hearted as he ever had been. At a glance Galton noticed that none of the furniture was familiar and all of it, at least the pieces in the drawing-room, were secondhand. The fine armchairs, the cabinet and the hardwood dining-table must have been sold to satisfy his creditors.

Jessie came out, wiping her hands on an apron she was wearing over her cotton dress.

"So you found the place at last," she said, advancing towards him.

Her face was drawn and her arms, exposed from the elbow down, were thin.

"Sit down, man," Winston urged him. "You heard what happened, eh? Selwyn told you? Boy! What a business! I can't even offer you rum, things're so bad. What about you?"

"Oh, all right," Galton said.

"It's true that you and Gemma . . . ?" asked Winston, purposely neglecting to finish his sentence.

"Yes."

"If it's not one thing it's the other, isn't it? Thelma!" he called out to his daughter. "Come and say hello. Where are your manners?"

"Thelma!" Jessie called in turn, and then went inside to get her.

Thelma came out, duly gave her hand and then retired promptly.

"She's worse than ever," said Winston in a low voice. "The Queen of silence. We're worried about her. . . ." Then, drawing closer, he said in a whisper, "She hasn't even got her periods yet, at her age. Would you believe it? That well developed frame doesn't mean a thing. She's driving everybody round the bend with her peculiar ways. The day I raise my hand to her I'll . . . !"

Galton had expected to find a depressed, uncommunicative Winston. To see him among the shabby furniture, ensconced in a Berbice chair that took up a fair proportion of his drawing-room, and holding forth in the same way as he used to do in the ample accommodation of his new house, was for him a revelation. Jessie used to complain that she had too little to do. Now, at eight o'clock, she was still working.

Jessie came out with a tray of soft drinks in the elegant glasses he knew they reserved for special guests. So they were allowed to keep those!

"You all right, Galton?" she enquired solicitously.

"Yes. You're working hard!"

"The washing," she said, with a faint smile. "I don't think I'll ever curse servants again. But things could be worse."

"For some time you didn't have one in our first place," Winston reminded her.

Jessie looked down at her husband, the picture of relaxation as he held her hand.

"Sit down, girl," Winston said to her.

"Everybody's not like you," she retorted, a touch of sourness in her voice; and she left the two men to go back to the kitchen.

They talked of old times, before they were married. They talked about everything except Galton's marriage and Winston's bankruptcy. Winston informed him that Jessie's mother had gone back to Golden Grove and that Jessie missed her sorely.

"Tell me," said Winston, looking into his friend's eyes. "Why did you go away without saying anything? All of a sudden, like that. Jessie never forgave you, y'know."

Galton was so confused that Winston came to his rescue.

"And you didn't even leave your address. . . . Drink up and let Thelma get us some more. We don't have a fridge now and if you don't buy ice early you suffer for the rest of the day."

"Don't bother," said Galton. "Soft drinks only make me thirsty."

"Look," said Winston, "say something to Thelma about school for me. She just won't work. The trouble started when we moved here. She can't accept the fact that we've come down in the world."

"You mean she can't accept the fact that her face is covered with pimples," Galton remarked, seized with a desire to be offensive.

Winston, surprised at the remark, was now certain that Galton believed himself the victim of some fancied wrong.

"You may be right," Winston agreed. "It was soon after we came here that they came out. They're a sight, eh? We're so accustomed to them we don't notice any more. Well, you're going to talk to her?"

Galton nodded. Winston, instead of calling out, went himself to fetch Thelma. They could be heard bickering from the drawing-room. Presumably Thelma was protesting. When they finally came out she was pouting and, on approaching Galton gave him a cut-eye, which told him at once what she thought of his role as adviser.

"Sit down," Galton said to her.

She complied, deliberately choosing a chair some distance from him.

"How're you getting on at school?"

"Badly," came the answer.

"Why? You don't like school?"

"No."

"Why?"

She shrugged her shoulders.

"What's your best subject?" Galton enquired.

"Nothing!" she exclaimed, in an attempt to bring the pointless conversation to an end.

Galton smiled at her and asked, "How're your pimples?"

The question had the effect of an unexpected bullet on a herd of bush hogs. She jumped up from her seat and flounced off inside.

"What you had to ask her that for?" asked Winston. "She won't come out again for the rest of the night."

Winston looked at his friend closely and observed. "You've changed."

"How?" Galton asked eagerly.

"I dunno. Well, you've become more touchy, for one."

"Touchy?"

Galton then fell silent, as if lost in thought.

Then, as an afterthought, "And what else?"

"It's hard to say," Winston said. "Probably it's my imagination. You remember the talks we used to have before you were married? Everything looked as if it would last. You were going to be a bachelor for ever and I was going to accumulate property. But I'm not finished yet. They haven't heard the last of me." The last sentence was spoken half in jest and half in earnest.

"What you intend to do?" asked Galton.

"I'll wait until this bankruptcy thing is over and then I'll start again. Not as a butcher. You have to rely on too many people. When they see you getting somewhere they raise the price of their pigs. That might be the answer: keep my own pigs. You'll see!"

Galton found Winston's optimism irritating.

"You see it in simple terms," he said.

"All success begins with a dream," Winston declared. "But you're right in a way. I'm too damned honest. The next time things'll be different."

"You're just as intellectual as ever," observed Galton. "For me life hasn't got dreams, success and all that damn nonsense. Life is full of shadows: some of them are soft and others conceal a hammer."

"And how d'you know which is which?" asked Winston, perturbed by Galton's intense expression.

"You don't! That's it!" declared Galton.

"You mean to say that disaster is a hit and miss affair."

"I don't know what you mean by disaster. Life itself is a disaster," said Galton emphatically.

Jessie came out, wearing wet rubber gloves. She put a finger to her lips and pointed to the bedroom.

"Keep your voices down," she whispered. "It's not a conversation for Thelma."

She went back to her work, uneasy in the knowledge that when her husband and Galton were together they invariably got involved in a serious discussion and forgot about everything else around them.

"This damn house!" Winston exclaimed. "There's no privacy. . . . Now, you're saying life is one long disaster. . . ."

And so they talked for hours until the kitchen light went out and there was silence in the house except for their own talking. The hired cars had stopped running and the buses. Galton went off in the direction of Georgetown, several miles away. He passed the house where, as a boy, he had spent three weeks while his mother was ill, three weeks in the house of a distant relation. The back yard, dotted with houses, was full of children in the afternoons. It was there he had learnt to make and spin a buck top which sang and droned until, losing speed, it fell over. There he had got stained with a beer, the red water thrown indiscriminately during the East Indian Phagwah festival. The East Indian women used to suckle their infants on the stairs in full view of everyone, and when he went home and told his mother this she punished him and made him say a prayer in which he asked to be forgiven for his evil thoughts. Then there was the cake shop with its sloping wooden bridge high above the gutter. He had never seen such an assortment of cakes in his life, all costing just three cents each. How much time he had spent on the bridge on the warm afternoons, gawking at the cakes in the glass case when the proprietress was asleep. There were butter-flap, Chinee cake, white eye, collar, pine tart, pone, conkee and others, strewn at random on the oily brown paper. In the nights he used to sit at the window, longing for home, his boredom often relieved by the talk of the young men. Before he could understand what all their words meant he had learnt about various love positions, like the crab and the bull poop, in which the woman's legs were splayed high against the wall. All this was heady stuff for a boy who was not permitted out to play except with his brother or the express permission of his mother.

As Galton walked on, his thoughts became more sombre. Of late he was dogged by the belief that he was in a bottle and was afraid that if he fell asleep someone would come and insert a cork in its mouth, leaving him imprisoned. Once, he even thought he had caught a glimpse of the person waiting in the shadows to catch him asleep, but could not recall his features. His insomnia had returned, and the sleep that came about two hours before he had to get up was no longer deep, but fitful and full of fantasies. Whether it was his growing fatigue or the thought of walking all the way to Georgetown and across it that depressed him, Galton was unable to say. The fact was that he wished passionately to be back in the flat and to throw himself on his bed.

When the curve of La Penitence bridge appeared in the dark he increased the length of his step. He knew he could not face the rest of the journey to Kitty and hoped that the watchman would be on night duty. There was no light and the bench in front of the sawmill was deserted.

"Anybody?" he called.

For some while there was no response, but just as Galton was about to call out again the watchman appeared.

"Ah, is you? You on days? What you doing down hey at this time? You off tomorrow?"

Galton did not reply. He sat down on the bench.

"Sit down, ne," Galton told his friend. "I've got something to tell you."

"Something happen?" asked the watchman, alarm in his voice.

Galton gave his friend a long, searching look, then declared, "I killed Gemma."

The watchman crossed himself.

"Jus' now?" he asked.

"No. The time when I told you she left me."

Some moments went by before the watchman said. "All this time."

Galton opened the two top buttons of his shirt.

"Well, if you can keep it all this time I hope you in' going tell nobody else now," said the watchman. "*She* know?"

"Who?" Galton asked.

"The new one. Mildred."

"She? No, she doesn't know."

"You in' going tell she?"

"No. . . . I bet you didn't think I could . . . snuff out a life, eh? I bet I surprised you," said Galton, and thereupon gave a short, humourless laugh.

"My boy, me oldest one," said the watchman, "he went to his brother wife and tell she that she husband got a woman outside. He do that, and he was the best of me sons, the most honest and. . . . You. . . . No. I din' think you could kill anybody. But listen to me, boy: you not well. I been talking to the wife and she say she don't mind you coming and living there. But now I going have to tell she 'bout this and. . . . What you want me to say, Galton? I in' got nothing to say. You shouldn'a tell me. Murder! Why you do it?"

"We were going to separate. She wanted her independence."

"Boy, you should have gone back to the bush long ago and marry a Buck girl. They mek good wives. The trouble is . . . the trouble is . . . . What you going do? You still got time. Go back to the bush. . . . don' think you ever been so content as when you been there. I lie? Go on, I lying?"

"No. I suppose it's true," replied Galton.

"Course is true. That's why you don't talk 'bout it . . . I got a mind to come wit' you, but I think I past it."

The two men sat hunched forward on the bench.

"How it happen?" the watchman asked.

Galton did not reply immediately.

"She went down to the water with me. I took her down to the water and hit her over the head with a piece of wood."

"Jesus Christ, boy. That woman would'a mek you do all the things you did want to do. I must admit I never could understand you."

"You're wrong, you see. I'm sick, but she was even more sick. It's this bottle. You dare not go to sleep."

"Which bottle?" asked the watchman.

"Don't be a damn fool, man. Can you go to sleep without worrying about the cork?"

"You're right!" the older man said, trying to humour him. He remembered how Galton had raved when he said Gemma had gone away. This time the captain was not in port. If, then, he had suspected the cause of Galton's behaviour he would have put a great deal of distance between them. The phase had passed. Why should it not pass this time?

"How's Mildred?" enquired the watchman.

"You asked already!" Galton exclaimed. "What you want to pry for? Let me give you her address if you're burning to know so!"

Galton fumbled in his pocket for a pen or a pencil.

"Don't bother. I tek you word for it," the watchman assured him.

"Of course you take my word for it. My word is as good as your word!" he shrieked.

"You all right?" a voice came from across the road.

"Yes, man," called out the watchman. "Is only me and me friend having a argument."

Galton was panting, as if he had been running.

"Why you don't lie down," proposed the watchman, "and go to sleep? I think you tired, that's all. In the morning if you don't feel like going to work I going say you had a accident."

Galton followed his friend to the back where the latter laid out a mat on a low pile of planks which had been put for delivery. Fatigued after the long walk, Galton was soon breathing deeply.

The watchman was frightened out of his wits. Perhaps Galton had killed this Mildred as well. He was certainly not going to give him away; but what if he attacked him? He had confessed to killing Gemma with a piece of wood. If he did not kill him it would not be for a lack of wood! For long he had suspected that Galton was mad, but now there was no doubt about it.

"Tcha! All this time he never touch a hair of my head. Why should he do it now?" he thought.

Had it not been for his wife he was sure he could get him back on the rails again; but he could not run the risk of taking him home. Galton had something against women, without doubt, for not once had he spoken well of his mother, of his sister-in-law . . . and poor Gemma. Yet there was this Mildred, who had brought the light back into his eyes. If only he could find out where she lived he might talk to her and ask her to help—if he had not yet done away with her as well.

These young people of today, he thought, with their fear of responsibility. Galton had covered most of his radio course in a short time; he had married a solid, hard-working woman; he had a half share in a cottage with land round it. What more could a young man want these days?

"Suppose he'd had *my* life?" said the watchman to himself.

The watchman woke Galton just before dawn and saw him cross the road and walk further on to the mill where he worked.

TWENTY-THREE

That evening Nekka put her head out of the window as Galton was opening the gate.

"Two men come to see you. As you back door wasn't locked I let them in."

"Thanks," he muttered.

She smiled back at him and withdrew. He then opened the door of his flat and entered the drawing-room.

"Eh, Galton. It's a long time."

It was his father-in-law. When Galton saw a man come out of his kitchen he gave a start. He immediately recognised him as the man he had seen the night when he went back to the ramp, when it was raining.

"This is the person I was telling you about," Mr Burrowes added, "who did so much for Gemma. You know . . . her godfather."

Galton, enraged that a stranger had made himself at home in his flat and had not even bothered to apologise when he walked in, looked the man up and down and said, "I don't know you. What're you doing in my house?"

The stranger's expression became grave and he looked at Mr Burrowes, who declared, "Galton, I told you who this is. I'm sorry if. . . . He only went to the latrine."

Galton realised that he had misunderstood.

"What d'you want?" he asked gruffly.

"Do you mind if we sat down?" said Mr Burrowes.

Galton made a gesture, indicating that he did not mind if his father-in-law sat down.

"You heard anything more about Gemma?" enquired Mr Burrowes's friend.

"No. And you?" asked Galton.

"I haven't heard anything," he declared in turn.

"Why don't you go to the police again?" Galton asked his father-in-law.

This suggestion seemed to annoy him.

"I wrote you why," he replied.

"But after such a long time they might be prepared to do something."

"Mm," he muttered. "We prefer to settle it with you. Y'see, Galton, Mr Giles," and here Mr Burrowes nodded towards his friend, "is the father of Gemma's child."

No emotion, Galton kept repeating to himself. Then aloud, "Why d'you tell me that now, eh? Why you didn't say that when you first came to see me?"

Gemma's father turned towards Mr Giles as if expecting him to come to his rescue, but the latter did not interfere.

"The Walk-Man warned me about you, but you said he was a liar," Galton observed.

At the mention of the Walk-Man, Mr Giles appeared to listen attentively.

"So you met him?" asked Mr Giles. "He's my brother."

"And I was suspicious of him. Hm!" exclaimed Galton. "Every word he spoke was true. Every word. Then he wouldn't say any more because I behaved like a pig at his table. It's such a long time ago, I can't remember."

"You've ever woken up and found yourself in a bottle?" he asked aloud, looking at them in turn.

"Not often, no," replied Mr Giles sarcastically.

"In a bottle full of lies? Crawling all over it? And then, suddenly, Ph! The cork is stuck in it and you're trapped."

"This is no time for jokes. We know what you've done to Gemma!" his father-in-law exclaimed.

"Know? What does a bumpkin like you know? You mean you suspect. *I* know. And *he*," said Galton, pointing to Mr Giles, "*thinks* he knows. A man lives in Wismar and finds himself in Georgetown at the very moment I go down to one of the scores of ramps along the river, when the rain is pouring so hard that no one is out on the road. No one was sheltering in the vicinity. You explain that. Explain something else: A woman marries a man without telling him she's got a child and this same woman, in cold blood, demands her independence. . . . She must've wanted to die."

"You admit you killed her, then?" the godfather hastened to ask Galton.

"You don't understand. I don't admit it. I *proclaim* it. Gemma wasn't fit to live."

"That's what we came here for, Mr Flood. You understand," said Mr Giles, without any trace of anger. "All I want is to see you hang."

"Now, if you had come alone," retorted Galton, "we would've had a lot to talk about. But you brought this clown, this degenerate who couldn't even take care of his own daughter, and thinks he's got the right to point a finger at me."

"Look here," said Mr Burrowes angrily, but at the same time wary of Galton's aggressive behaviour.

"Don't let's quarrel," said Mr Giles quietly. "Did you throw her into the river?"

Galton reflected that in some strange way Mr Giles resembled the watchman.

"What's your name again?" Galton asked him.

"Giles. Therphilio Giles," he answered courteously.

He got up and shook Galton's hand.

"Now, Mr Flood. Would you care to tell us how you killed Gemma?"

"Yes. I hit her over the head with a piece of wood and she fell into the river. I then tied strips of lead round her body and eased it over the ramp."

Mr Giles noticed Gemma's father's agitation, but pressed on.

"At the spot where you dipped your hand in the water?" Mr Giles asked.

"Yes," Galton answered, as docile as a lamb.

"One more thing, Galton. Do you mind me calling you Galton?" he enquired, tending Galton a cigarette.

"Thanks, no. I roll mine."

"Sorry," Mr Giles smiled, "I prefer the manufacturers to do the work."

"But you pay for it," Galton reminded him.

"So I do, so I do. . . . Mm, after we've finished talking, perhaps you'd have dinner with me. It's my second visit to Georgetown, you know, and it's like a long dream. Anyhow, there's one more thing I'd like you to do for me. If you don't mind, of course. Can you write down what you said to me and sign it? You know, the weapon you used, how you weighted the body down and where you threw it in."

Galton hesitated.

"Galton," said Mr Giles, "you're not obliged to do it. If you don't, my invitation to dinner still stands. I abhor force, you see, or even persuasion."

Galton recalled Gemma's description of her seduction by this man with the honey-tongued speech and yellow teeth; how he waited until the moment was ripe. If she knew how envious he was of him, of his ability to deal with women.

"Will you write it?" asked Mr Giles, taking a pen out of his new shirt-jack and offering it to Galton.

"No, I won't write it."

"Very well, Galton," he said, after a moment's hesitation. He then replaced the pen in his pocket and stood up. "I'm ready if you are."

"Come into the kitchen," Galton said to Mr Giles, "I want to talk to you."

They left Mr Burrowes alone in the larger room.

"You're interested in what I did," began Galton. "But I'm just as interested in you. I've lain awake at nights thinking of you, envying you. You assed up my life by doing what you did to Gemma, yet would you believe it, I feel so close to you. . . . Did she enjoy it with you?"

"She must have done," answered Mr Giles in his unruffled manner.

"Ah, how sure you are of yourself. Oh, my God! How you're sure. Gemma said I was good-looking; she called me her intellect and yet I was never sure of her, nor did she spare me for all that. Tell me: suppose Gemma had asked you for her independence what would you've done?"

Mr Giles, suddenly overwhelmed with pity for Galton, answered, "I would've given it to her; she wouldn't have taken it."

Galton grasped his hand and shook it vigorously. "I knew it," he said. "But I couldn't help myself. The trouble is they never buried my mother, but she doesn't persecute him," and in saying this he lifted his head to indicate the flat above them.

Galton turned away abruptly and rejoined his father-in-law in the next room.

Without a word he led the two men out and locked the front door. Then, remembering that the back door was open, he went round the side of the house and closed it.

"I now see why people who leave Wismar to come to Georgetown never go back," said Mr Giles, on seeing an attractive woman walk by.

"The last time you came to see me," Galton told Gemma's father, "you were waiting in my room. The tenant who let you in is a police informer. This time you were let in by my sister-in-law, who's a rat. You've got a way with people of a certain breed, haven't you?"

Gemma's father halted. "You animal!" he exclaimed, but mastered his indignation quickly.

Galton halted at the bus stop.

"Let's walk," suggested Mr Giles. "We mustn't waste a pleasant night like this. I came through a Peter Rose Street, somewhere but—"

"Peter Rose Street? We've got to turn down that way," said Galton.

The three men went along the new pavements, turned into Queenstown and walked along Lamaha Street, lined with elegant houses of the new aristocracy and the embassies, until they reached Peter Rose Street. Mr Giles, enthralled by what he saw, slowed down now and then to look up at some house that caught his fancy.

Galton stopped all at once.

"I can't eat with you," he said abruptly.

"Why?" asked his father-in-law.

But Galton had already begun to walk in the opposite direction.

"Animal!" his father-in-law shouted after him.

On reaching home he went and knocked on his brother's door. Selwyn himself opened.

"Why you didn't come in? You knocked as if you're a stranger," he chided his younger brother.

"Nekka there?" Galton asked.

"Yes. Is anything wrong?" Selwyn enquired.

"I just want to ask her something," Galton said.

"Galton wants to see you," Selwyn called out.

Selwyn's little boy was sitting on his high chair, fidgeting with both hands.

"Mammy! Uncle want you!" he shouted, banging his spoon on his plate.

"I coming! Stop it or you go'n break the plate!" she shouted in turn.

Nekka took some time to come out and when she finally did Galton said, "Why did you let those two men into my flat?"

"The back door wasn't lock; I tell you," she answered.

"How did you know?" he asked, almost triumphantly.

"Galton, you leave it open a lot of times. Ask Selwyn."

"Why?" enquired Selwyn. "Who're the two men?"

"If you ever put your fingers on that door again, I'll break your neck, understand?" he threatened.

"You're talking to my wife, Galton," Selwyn objected.

"I don't care who she is. Where the hell did she get a key to my flat?"

"It was open, I tell you," she insisted.

"Then how did they get in?" Galton asked again.

"Christ!" Selwyn exclaimed in despair. "You go inside," he ordered Nekka, doing his best to remain calm.

"What's wrong, Galton? Sit down, ne? Did they take anything?"

But Galton just stood there staring after his sister-in-law, who had done as Selwyn asked.

"Your wife spread lies about me round the neighbourhood," Galton said in Selwyn's ear.

"I told you it wasn't her fault about Mildred. . . ."

"Talk into my ear," proposed Galton. "I don't want to complain. I prefer to deal with matters myself. But I just wanted you to know in case she goes spreading lies about you. That woman down the road doesn't speak to me any more because of her—what's her name?"

"Mildred."

"Yes. . . . Ah! That's her name, eh? You see, one day I was talking to her and the next I wasn't."

"Brother, listen to me," began Selwyn. "You trust me, don't you? Come, come." Then he called out to his wife: "I won't be long, Nekka."

Selwyn put his arm through his brother's, led him out of the house and made him take a seat next to him in his car.

"Where're we going?" asked Galton.

"Don't you trust me? Remember how we used to play marbles and you always beat me? Remember?"

Selwyn reversed over the bridge and turned the car towards Vlissingen Road.

"Where're we going? I'm hungry," Galton complained.

"All right, let's go and see the doctor quickly and we can come back and eat. . . ."

"The who? You've ever known me to be sick? Man, it's been more than twenty-one years since I've been sick."

"Galton. . . ."

"Stop!" Galton shouted, and Selwyn pulled up at once.

Galton jumped out of the car and went back home on foot. Selwyn would have gone to fetch the doctor himself, but remembered that his wife and children were alone in the house. He managed to turn in the narrow road and got back just before Galton.

Selwyn locked and bolted both doors and waited. Nekka, on learning that Galton was probably mad, reproached her husband for building the flat for him.

"I did tell you, but you wouldn't listen. What I going do tomorrow with only the servant? Suppose he come up and attack the children? You got to get he certified."

"No! If he goes he'll never come back!" exclaimed Selwyn.

"What you going do then? Answer, ne? You got two children. There's no madness in my family; I not accustom to—"

Selwyn, angry at her jibe, said, "There's no madness, but there's crass stupidity. You're going on like this in front of the child."

"Tell me then what I going do tomorrow?"

"I don't know yet. I'll work out something."

Selwyn decided that it would not be a good idea to telephone the doctor, for, if his own diagnosis were to be confirmed, Galton would be sent away.

They waited until midnight, when Nekka retired. Selwyn then went downstairs to make another effort to speak to his brother, but he had gone out.

Galton had, in fact, left soon after he came back. During the hours that Selwyn and Nekka had been waiting anxiously to see what he would get up to he was pounding the streets. He had first gone to look up the watchman; but on being told that it was his day off Galton abused the man who had given him the information and called him a liar. He knew that the watchman was hiding and did not care to see him, he declared.

It was in the early hours of the morning that Selwyn and Nekka were awakened by a banging on the door.

"She's a snake, brother!" Galton's voice boomed through the jalousie. "When she's done with you you'll be like a mango, squeezed dry! And you will leave your ambition smeared on the floor of her house."

There was a scratching on the door, like that of a dog trying to get into a house where it was accustomed to sleep.

Nekka wanted to speak, but Selwyn put his hand over her mouth.

"I'm telling you, brother. The next time it rains don't take a bath, because the shower'll be dripping blood. Can't you see, brother? Everything was at an end long, long ago. . . . The next time it rains, brother, it won't stop and the world will come to an end."

The pounding began again and Selwyn got up carefully, so as to prevent the bed creaking.

"I know you're in there, Selwyn. You think I'm sick, but I've got things to tell you. It started when I had my first drink. You all didn't believe me when I talked about the bottle, did you? You know what a bottle's for? After all you're a dispenser. Don't you put poisons in a bottle? Well, answer me! Don't you? And what else? Of course! Alcohol! But there're other things that go into bottles, brother: Men! However, they don't come out, you see. The bocals of coloured water you leave in the window of your drug store have no life, but a man corked in a bottle. . . . Ah, brother! That Christmas when our mother tore down the bunting and trampled it under her feet; that was not nice; Father went out and she wouldn't let us wait up for him. Remember, brother? . . . It doesn't matter, because every Christmas we die a little."

His voice had fallen and Selwyn was sitting alone in the drawing-room, crying like a child. On hearing his brother going down the stairs he looked up, but remained sitting, and when Nekka came out to join him he sent her back to bed.

Galton was afraid to lie down, lest he should fall asleep and dream, and indeed, when he fell asleep in the wicker armchair he dreamt that he was at the edge of the ramp where he had struck Gemma. He was watching the water and felt the up-and-down motion of the ramp. Rain was threatening from low, slate-grey clouds, and a rank odour rose from the murky river. His eyes were riveted on the water when, suddenly, a hand rose from it, with groping fingers clawing after some object. Eventually the fingers touched the ramp and the hand, in a desperate grip, pulled on the ramp until another hand appeared, followed by a head and the rest of the body. Galton recognised the apparition as that of his mother. Instead of coming to him it went by, and when Galton looked round it was bringing down a stick with all its might on the head of a man who, streaming with blood, was looking to him for help. But it was when the man pleaded, "Galton!" that he recognised him as his father. Galton, moved to action by the sight of his father, open-mouthed, eyes staring in terror, sprang forward, only to run into a panel of thick glass, polished to such transparency that he was unable to see it in the half light. He made another effort to get past but to no avail. From behind the glass, which he began to pound furiously with his fists, he could only remain a powerless observer of his father's distress; and when the latter fell forward into the river his mother pursued him, hacking away with the stick.

The next morning Galton made no effort to go to work. He got up when the alarm sounded, took a shower, cleaned his teeth and made the morning meal. He then sat in a wicker chair, staring through the lattice-work, undisturbed by the noises of the day and the children scampering on the floor above, Nekka's impatient voice, the servant's arrival, the chatter of passing school children, the laughter of women crowding round the milkman, the high-pitched chanting of East Indian music from the new neighbours and the shrill cry of the kiskadee. Then came the evening with its soft, reassuring sounds and the owl's hooting that silenced all else.

It was the season when Christmas trees on the waste land opposite showered down their whirling seed wings just before the coming of the December rains, to take root in furrows and perish afterwards, engulfed by the shadows of the silk-cotton giants. The rain clouds that came in from the sea settled over the land like a forest of black umbrellas, shutting out the stars and the endless sky.

At about seven o'clock Galton got up to make his evening meal. When he was about to prepare for bed there was a knock on the door, a firm but polite knock that was neither Selwyn's nor Nekka's. On opening, he stood face to face with Mr Giles. He was alone and when Galton looked over his shoulder, said, "I'm alone. You don't mind?"

Galton let him go by.

"Yesterday," remarked Mr Giles, "you were so put out by your father-in-law I thought it might be better to come alone. I nearly regretted it, though; I almost lost my way."

Galton sat down in his wicker chair and Mr Giles drew up another.

"I brought something for you," the latter said, and gave Galton a bottle wrapped up in paper. "It's X-M ten-year-old. Your father-in-law said you don't drink, but rum is rum, isn't it?" Galton had placed the bottle at his feet and was staring straight ahead.

"I came to apologise," said Mr Giles. "For what I said yesterday—about wanting to see you hang. Isn't it strange how they hang the weaklings like us and the others go scot free? You said something yesterday and I'd like to know what you meant. You said, 'If you'd come alone we would've had a lot to talk about.' What did you mean? Look, try and tell me; it's important."

Galton maintained his silence.

"You know," said Mr Giles, changing the subject, "you can tell a lot about someone by the names he gives his children. My father called me 'Therphilio,' not caring that I'd have to drag that name through life like an embarrassingly large behind. He was vain. I bet the name Galton can tell a lot about the parents who named you. . . . I imagined you to be different . . . the man who married Gemma, overbearing . . . and yesterday, every weakness I found in you was like a triumph."

Galton looked at Mr Giles for a very long while before gazing out through the lattice-work once more.

"It's strange that yesterday you could've talked your head off; and now you're silent. If you want me to go away, you've only got to say so."

"Go away," said Galton, still looking straight ahead.

Mr Giles got up, turned round at the door and said, "Don't bother about your father-in-law; he's too afraid of the scandal to go to the police. And, besides, he never cared for her."

He then stepped out into the windless night, having opened and closed the door himself. Walking slowly at first, he lengthened his stride on approaching Peter Rose Street.

Galton, at the departure of Mr Giles, prepared for bed. He did not know that upstairs the family had spent a tense day, expecting trouble at any minute. Selwyn had telephoned the man who opened the drug store every day and sold at the counter, asking him to carry on without him. By night time both Nekka and Selwyn were irritable, especially as hardly any sound had come from downstairs, and it was difficult to tell if Galton was at home or had gone out. They listened intently after the arrival of Mr Giles, but heard as little then as before. Nekka was afraid of going to bed since it was likely that Galton would erupt early in the morning, as he had done the day before.

The next morning both of them woke up, bleary-eyed. Selwyn went downstairs and knocked on the back door of his brother's flat, but received no answer.

With the passing days Selwyn and Nekka gradually came to terms with Galton's condition and one Sunday as they were at table he appeared in the drawing-room. Nekka made an involuntary movement, pulling the younger child on her lap closer to her.

"What you want, Galton?" Selwyn asked, standing up and pushing his chair away from him.

"Can I borrow some food?" he asked.

"Sure, sure," Selwyn said, hurrying to comply.

"Not cooked food," said Galton.

"What?"

"Some rice and sugar and a bit of salt."

Selwyn got the things together and put them into a shopping bag, which he handed to Galton, who left by the front door.

Nekka wiped her child's face with its napkin, then threw the cloth down on the table angrily. She dared not say anything.

"At least he doesn't look dangerous," remarked Selwyn.

"No, but he in' going work if you feed him, is he?" she asked indignantly.

"We've got to give him time."

"All right, we going give him time and hope he don't set the house 'pon fire!"

•

Galton is a familiar figure about Georgetown, distinguished by his headband, his well-laundered clothes and his frequent cries of "Don't cork the bottle!" His favourite haunt is the Lombard Street district, where people are especially indulgent towards him. The first time he was found in the alley, staring up at the room where he once lived, someone pointed him out to a policeman, but in time it was accepted that he was harmless and had not once been seen there at night. He never answers anyone who speaks to him, even the watchman, whom he occasionally meets when he goes to a cook-shop in Lombard Street.

Selwyn gives Galton money to buy tobacco and food and takes his dirty garments to the laundry. Nekka once remarked that it is not his interest in Galton's welfare that causes him to do this, but his own vanity.

Jessie crosses to the other side of the road when she is in town and spots Galton from a distance. As for Mildred, she is mortally afraid of him ever since the day when she went up to ask how he was and he held her wrist in a tight grip and would not let go for a long time.

And often, as he sits alone in the cake-shop, it seems to Galton that he had lived in that quarter for a hundred years; that all the brooding of his childhood had fermented there, in the alleyway, in the passage guarded by the fat girl; that his ripening manhood was spent in that room beneath dust showers of books and dogs. The house in David Street was for sleeping, like a resting place among grass that claims no allegiance, or pylons in the rain.

His attachment is so strong that sometimes he gets up at two or three in the morning, dresses and makes for Lombard Street, a night bird in pursuit of brittle dreams. The streets then belong to him and waifs and solitary constables trying the padlocks of shuttered shop fronts.